Withdrawn

THE
LOSERS' CLUB

THE
LOSERS' CLUB

LISE S. BAKER

Thomas Dunne Books

St. Martin's Minotaur

New York

THOMAS DUNNE BOOKS.
An imprint of St. Martin's Press.

Copyright Acknowledgments:
From *Everest: The West Ridge* by Thomas Hornbein. Copyright ©
1965 by Thomas Hornbein. Reprinted with permission of Sierra Club
Books.

One More Try, by George Michael © 1988 Morrison-Leahy Music
Ltd. (ASCAP). All rights administered by Chappell & Co. (ASCAP).
All rights reserved. Used by permission. Warner Bros. Publications
U.S. Inc., Miami, FL 33014

Pink Houses, by John Mellencamp © 1983 EMI Full Keel Music. All
rights reserved. Used by permission. Warner Bros. Publications
U.S. Inc., Miami, FL 33014

Design by Maureen Troy

Library of Congress Cataloging-in-Publication Data
Baker, Lise S.
      The losers club / Lise S. Baker.—1st ed.
          p. cm.
      ISBN 0-312-24216-6
      1. Insurance investigators—Nevada—Fiction. 2. Women
detectives—Nevada—Fiction. 3. Nevada—Fiction. I. Title.

PS3552.A43147 L67 2000
813'.6—dc21
                                                      00-020336

10   9   8   7   6   5   4   3   2

F

For Truth, Justice,
and the American Way

Thanks and acknowledgments to:

B.S.B., for his Thanksgiving Day run over the Donner Summit

T.S.B., for trying to take notes heading up around the bend

Joe Renshaw, Bail Bonds Unlimited

Sandi, Department of Vital Statistics—
Washoe County, Reno, Nevada

Vernon McCarty, Coroner/Washoe County, Nevada

Dave McBride, PI, McBride & Associates

Dad and Mom, for urging me on and telling me I'm okay
(they're okay)

Melanie Fitzpatrick, The Typing Place

Art Martinez, PI, Ravenoaks Investigations

Les Roberts, my favorite judge

Ruth Cavin, a great editor

Don Maass, my literary agent

and a very special thanks to:

Joe Curtis, retired Carson City Sheriff's Dept.,
owner Mark Twain's Bookstore—Virginia City, Nevada.
Without Joe's input and insight this book would most
certainly not be the same (especially those jackalopes!).

THE
LOSERS' CLUB

PROLOGUE

NIGHT WAS DAY AND day was night as the crowd streamed in and out of the casino as if under a powerful sorcerer's spell. Scantily clad waitresses inhaled secondhand smoke from the tips of a thousand cigarettes glowing red like shipwreck flares. A cacophonous din of bells, buzzers, and shouts assaulted newcomers. Then, as they too became entranced, the noise blended into the backdrop of this raucous new world.

"Seven up!" A croupier's voice rose above the din, followed by a chorus of both groans and shrieks of delight. There was the steady clink of silver dollars and quarters and nickels as they spewed out of the slots and then there was the silent flow of dollar bills and fives and tens as the machines grabbed them up into their innards. A brand-new all-chrome Harley-Davidson motorcycle spun in a silvery circle on its perch, promising itself to the luckiest winner.

On the casino's second floor was a children's gaming arcade adjacent to the restaurant. The four-year-old boy coming down the escalator stared up at the top of the huge room's interior dome. A laser show was in full swing. The roaring thunder of audio split the air with crashing booms. The boy looked straight upward, oblivious to his surroundings; the lights and noise had his total attention.

On the escalator ahead of him was a blond woman in her mid-forties, sturdily built, more than a hint of muscle. An oversized brown teddy bear with a red ribbon tied around its neck had been placed in a stroller on the step below the blond. In back of the boy was a dark-complected woman carrying a tote bag. Neither one of the women looked at the boy, their eyes were fixed on some unseen horizon, their faces expressionless.

One of the roving cocktail waitresses, a redhead with short, curly hair and heavy eye makeup, paused in her serving as a patron meted out a tip. She idly scanned the crowd. Looking over at the escalator, she caught the flat stare of the dark-complected woman who, in turn, immediately frowned. The waitress took two steps back, startled.

Events happened quickly after that.

The stroller hit the unmoving end of the escalator first. The husky blond was jerked out of her reverie by its mild jarring motion and in response, stumbled. Her large, unyielding form was a barricade to the child, who immediately tumbled backward. The woman coming down in back of him instinctively thrust out her hands, pushing him back over, onto his side.

One moment orchestrated bedlam, the next—chaos.

The escalator quickly became a human domino game.

Other casino patrons either backed up or staggered and lost their balance. The blond woman had moved the stroller to one side but stood there, strangely immobile. A pit boss ran over and, encountering her first, tried to get around her. She was turned to stone, unyielding, monolithic.

He lurched between her and the escalator rail and hit the emergency button. The sudden stopping motion caused a few more screams and more people lost their footing. But not everyone in the casino realized the emergency situation erupting. Several hundred people were still engrossed in their machines or their games.

It only appeared in the small circle surrounding the child that things had gotten very, very quiet.

The boy had been wearing a nylon windbreaker and the top string around his throat had gotten stuck, actually caught up, in the metal teeth of the escalator. Intense pressure had immediately been put on the small throat.

Regarding the child with a preternatural calm, the blond appeared to be assessing the situation rather than reacting to it. Then she let out a low keening. As her gaze met the dark-skinned woman's, she immediately fell silent, shut off as if she had been slapped.

"The stroller should not have been brought on the escalator," the pit boss chided the woman, not yet seeing the boy's face. The blond's passivity became a target for his ire.

A Willie Nelson look-alike sprang out of the crowd and ran toward the tableau. "Get back!" he yelled, a large hunting knife in one hand.

The pit boss's face went through several seconds of

3

stunned changes. It was all happening too fast, way too fast. That was when he saw the child's face: swollen, blue, every mother's nightmare. He moved aside and the gray-haired man with the ponytail and Bowie knife bent over the boy.

"Call 911. Has anybody called 911?" A woman's voice rose above the din.

"What is it? What's going on?" Another voice.

"I can't see. Can't—a big crowd over there—there—"

"The stroller, the stroller—" The pit boss was down on his knees.

The big blond's eyes were as glassy as the brown bear's; she hadn't moved—an Easter Island artifact, a pillar of salt. The dark-skinned woman stood on the outer fringe of the crowd, almost melting back into it.

Sirens.

From the far reaches of the room bells went off; someone had hit a big one. Their ship had come in; their lucky day had arrived. Salvation in the room with no clocks, the room with no windows.

Sirens from far away, coming closer and closer, until all at once, they died out.

Confusion reigned for quite some time. It was nearly two hours later when two kitchen workers, taking a smoke break in the odorous alley, saw the waxen white hand sticking out from behind one of the garbage cans. The short-order cook went over and moved the can.

"My God!"

It was one of the cocktail waitresses. His words caught in his throat as he felt vainly for a pulse.

The victim's heavily made-up eyes, which were still open, stared blindly, a horrible, startled expression stamped upon them.

The way down and the way up
are one and the same.

—HERACLITUS

And there's winners
and there's losers
But they ain't no big deal

—JOHN MELLENCAMP

1

THERE WAS LONELINESS, TOO, AS THE SUN SET, BUT ONLY RARELY NOW DID DOUBTS RETURN. THEN I FELT SINKINGLY AS IF MY WHOLE LIFE LAY BEHIND ME. ONCE ON THE MOUNTAIN I KNEW (OR TRUSTED) THAT THIS WOULD GIVE WAY TO TOTAL ABSORPTION WITH THE TASK AT HAND. BUT AT TIMES I WONDERED IF I HAD NOT COME A LONG WAY ONLY TO FIND THAT WHAT I REALLY SOUGHT WAS SOMETHING I HAD LEFT BEHIND.

SPRAWLED ON THE SEAT in the surveillance van, Cal Brantley read the paragraph over and over. Hornbein's words from *Everest: The West Ridge* held a key, a clue, to what had formed unsaid over the last months in her own thoughts. But what to do about it? What further action could she take?

She was as far from Mt. Everest as she could get but somehow she was mentally on a kind of par with the climber. Truths or illusions? She remembered reading somewhere that losing an illusion made you wiser than finding a truth. What was it that made truths shine so much more brilliantly on the pages of a book?

The shadow lady (as she thought of herself) sighed, her actions unseen, unheard. Being in that van was like living a subterranean existence. Where had the very air gone, the sun? It was for those that she followed, in many ways freer than she was. The peak of her being was to catch them doing a veritable slate of sins. Sins as defined by yet another group. The author, Orwell, of course was right but it had really gone a step further. Big Brother for big cash.

That was her Everest.

Cal's gaze flickered back and forth between the words on the page and the house she was watching. Three weeks she had been here and zero results. *Nada*. She had long gotten over attempting to will something to happen. It wasn't her life; she was only an onlooker. Onlooking.

She read the last sentence over and over again, not daring to take her eyes off the house for more than a few moments. Things could happen in the wink of an eye. Things you couldn't explain away to a client. "They must have come out the other exit," or "I had to go to the bathroom," were non sequiturs in the sleuth world. Zero results, zero excuses. And bet on it, no paying of the bill.

Wink of an eye. Maybe it was just that—the total concentration was driving her crazy, so crazy she identified more with high altitude sickness, supplemental oxygen, and base camps perched on jagged horizons. The waiting could do that to a surveillance operative, the waiting and the extremes. One minute practically comatose, the next second, heart pounding into overdrive, doing what could only be called a

Steve McQueen chase scene up and down the hills of San Francisco.

Surreptitiously of course.

It was foolhardy, absolutely nuts to do a one-man, or in this case, one-woman, surveillance in this city. Every sub rosa had its problems, its obstacles. From hiding your van in a vacant lot to trailer parks where everyone seemed to be on the lam and the lookout. But the client didn't care. They wanted the job done and done right. Zero tolerance.

One person on a case in San Francisco—off to a bad start. But the client had elected to do just that.

Cal tried to look at the bright side. She could actually stretch her legs out today, an absolute luxury after yesterday. She had switched cars this morning and was using the "official" van. She didn't like using the van because she felt it stood out, fairly screaming, Cal thought, "look at me, I'm watching you!" Sitting there, hour after hour feeling more exposed by the second, not wanting to get burned, a fate even worse than losing the prey.

Yesterday she had used her own car, a Firebird. Fitting in, blending with the neighborhood cars, a little down-at-the-heels patina of dust helping obscure its truer purpose: spy-mobile. And at one point when the subject had made an innocent on-foot excursion to the local market, no one had paid Cal any attention. A man in a car slowly cruising—that would have drawn a stare, but a woman in a Berkeley sweat-shirt—not a glance. A genuine nonperson.

The client was a millionaire who wanted to watch his

fiancée. He'd rather know now than after the marriage, even though there was a tight prenuptial.

"Get more of a retainer," Cal had called Glenn Starzsinszky in the Glendale home office. "Three weeks without a move on the lady's part. Something doesn't feel right."

"Can't get through to the man," Glenn said, "I keep getting his male secretary."

"Twenty-five hundred's a drop in the bucket for the hours I'm putting in," Cal said. "Why didn't he authorize a two-man anyway?"

"Don't know. Said he thought we could handle it. And you have, haven't you?"

"I'm making good money. But I hate to see the company get burned on this one. And I don't know, I keep getting that hinky feeling."

"Okay. Let's call it off. I don't like it, yeah, you're right, Cal. Client's been so out of touch he'll be even harder to get hold of when the rest of the tab arrives."

"Tell the secretary we've come up with nada and we're pulling off till we get the go-ahead from the *man*."

"Sounds like a plan."

"Oh, *yeah*."

That was yesterday, today was right now.

And Cal sat there with nothing but the gut feeling (or was it hunger?) that she should be there. Something in the air (static electricity?), and it was feeling better than it had all week. Sheer craziness induced by oxygen deprivation?

Breathe in and out, she reminded herself. *You're on your own dime now.*

Six o'clock on a Friday. "Get a life, Cal Brantley," Cal said aloud in a rather unkind tone. "You, me, all of us." Then she felt her breath sharply catch as the front door opened. *Showtime.* Cal thought it now. Even a syllable aloud would have been diversion.

The subject rushed out, alone. Huge pink Velcro rollers adorned her head like fat sausages. A quick dash to the mailbox; the subject didn't look anywhere up and down the street.

Like she knew, Cal thought, *that I wouldn't be there.*

The woman hurried back to the house.

What's the rush, bub?

Cal's hands automatically reached for the camcorder.

Things happened really quickly after that. A taxi pulled up to the curb. Out jumped a man, midthirties, overnight bag in one hand.

One, two, three seconds, front door opening, in like Flynn. Door closed.

Her mind flashed. Didn't Glenn say "male secretary"?

Gotcha.

Everest, summiting.

2

"**YOU'RE GOING TO PAY** me for today, right?" Cal spoke on the car phone with Fred Underhill as she maneuvered through traffic. She was unprepared for the serious note in his voice.

"There could be problems," he responded.

"You're putting me on, right, Fred?"

"Officially, you're not working. Today was your day off."

"Well, maybe I'll just turn around and sell this tape to Daddy Warbucks." Cal definitely didn't like the way this conversation was going. Never one for keeping a low profile, she told Fred directly. "What's going on, Fred? You don't sound right."

"Just come into the office."

"I just finished a three-week Mexican standoff, pulled the entire thing out of the garbage can, and all you can say is come into the office?"

"Just—"

"Okay, I'm on my way in, but—"

"No buts, okay?" Fred sounded like the grim reaper if the reaper ever spoke.

Cal felt like she was a convict who had been let out of prison only to find that once back on the outside she was totally invisible. Elation was swiftly sinking, along with the setting sun in the West. Friday night too, and the verdict on the state of the Cal-nation was one word—alone.

She tried not to let all of her exasperation out. "It's too neat. Too pat. We pull off officially and lover boy shows."

"But—" Fred said.

Cal cut him short. "This was a setup, Fred. Why aren't you backing me? I'll need a photo of the client's male secretary for possible positive ID. And for the life of me, I don't know why you're—you're—" Cal didn't finish the sentence as she slowed to make a left onto Van Ness. There was a yield sign for her lane of traffic, which jutted around a small concrete pedestrian island. "I'm jazzed. I don't know about you, but I'm jazzed."

All lanes of oncoming traffic were heavy and she prepared to stop by slowing even more. She was turned slightly to the left, looking over her shoulder when there was a tremendous crash. The wrenching sound of metal and tinkling spray of breaking glass sounded far away but at the same time close, disturbingly close. The force of the collision had been so great a part of her mind refused to register it.

"Damn it!" Cal yelled. She shut off the engine and vaulted out of her company van. The car hadn't hit her squarely in the back, but had swerved as if to pass and smashed her on the rear left. Cal was stunned.

Fred's voice squeaked out of the car phone in her hand but she couldn't place the sound. She felt detached, but everything came into sharp focus. Too sharp. Two men were in the car that had hit her, gaping at her with antagonistic expressions through their cracked windshield. The car they were in was an older compact without a discernible color. No one appeared to have hit their heads on the windshield. It was probable, reasoned Cal, that the windshield was cracked before the collision. She was too numb to speak for several more seconds and stared back at the passenger in the front seat.

She walked over to the driver's side, and asked, "You okay?"

"You move your car, please, so I can get around," he said.

"You got insurance?"

He shook his head.

"Fred, Fred, are you still there?" Cal addressed the phone as if it was her only friend.

"Yeah, I'm here. What's going on? Are you all right? I thought I heard a crash."

"I've been hit!"

"Are you hurt?"

"I'm walking and talking. Call 911 for me. I can't write! I'm shaking. No pen. No paper. Here's their license number. No, wait, I'll call them. Wait, take down the license in case they take off before I have a chance—" Cal read it off to him. "Gotta go now. You're waiting for me. Good." Cal disconnected. Abruptly.

Friday night traffic in the city seemed like a surreal scene down the rabbit hole with Alice. Cars snaked by, everyone gawking, eyes wide, curious, staring. Traffic lights changed: red, green, yellow, red, green, yellow. The colors were fluid, sensuous, riotously kaleidoscopic. Horns blared.

"You move your car now?" the driver leaned out of his window.

"I don't know where you think you're going, mister, but you're going to stay here until the police arrive. We're all going nowhere."

At that very moment Cal felt that she had uttered the truth of the day, surpassing even Hornbein.

"See what I'm dialing? 911." Cal dialed with shaking fingers. "I've just been in a car accident. Two men are in the other car and they want to take off." Cal listened for a moment, then again read off the plate number. "Are you hurt?" she asked the other driver, who said no. "No ambulance, no. Okay."

Cal shut off the phone. "You're not going to make this a hit-and-run because they have your plate now."

A woman driver directly behind the car that had rear-ended Cal was edging her way around the debris. It had only been a few minutes but to Cal it seemed as if she had been there for a very long time. "Wait, wait," Cal called to her as she drove up on the sidewalk with one tire, eyeing Cal all the while as if she had a Third World disease. "Stop, please stop. You saw the whole thing. You're a witness." The woman kept on going.

"Do you have a driver's license?" Cal asked the driver, who had gotten out of his car. He was short, thin, and very young. Adjusting his glasses that kept slipping down his nose, he shook his head as he assessed the damage to both vehicles. A cold wind cut through the thin cotton of Cal's sweatshirt. Her nose had started to run and she longed to wipe it on a tissue. She felt exposed, naked, there on that street corner for all the staring eyes to see. Her mind seethed with disgust. An uninsured motorist! A possible hit-and-run! This was everything she came up against in her professional life.

If the driver had chosen to flee, Cal had seen the aftermaths of such incidents. Many times, the driver or owner denied knowing anything about the accident. They even reported the car stolen.

Cal thought of the other possible inequities of the system. Many times hit-and-run victims could not even get the license plates or only were able to get a partial. Then the accident was charged to their collision coverage—a chargeable accident if the hit-and-run was not provable!

"Where's your driver's license?" she demanded a second time. She wanted to get as much ID on him as she could in case he still decided to leave the scene. It was rush hour and the police might take quite a while to get there. Cal's resolve grew stronger. If there was one thing in the world she wouldn't become, it was a victim.

"My wallet was stolen," the driver said sadly; he had an accent, Russian perhaps.

"You hit me at forty-five miles an hour," Cal said, "and you have no insurance!"

"You—you stop suddenly." There, he was actually accusing Cal.

"Don't you know what the word *yield* means? It means to stop or slow. Yield, you know, to oncoming traffic." Cal didn't like the looks of the passenger who had gotten out of the car and was standing next to the driver. She had seen that look in the eyes of a great many people when she had lived in Miami. "I sue you now," it said.

"We're late," the passenger said in an irritated tone.

"Are you done with me now?" the driver said. "We're late for registration."

"I hope it's registration for driving school," said Cal. She glanced across the street. A man standing on the corner had to her an ominous interest in the situation.

"But you stop suddenly," the driver persisted.

"Tell it to the police." Cal figured the best defense was to be offensive. Nice guys didn't finish. "Look at what you did to my van."

"Look at what you did to my car," he said.

"How old are you anyway?" Cal asked.

"Sixteen."

"You got a green card?"

"It was in the wallet—"

"That was stolen. I got your number every which way. But you're not shaking loose."

"You move your car," said the passenger.

"Did you ever see that movie, *The Day the Earth Stood Still*?" Cal asked.

"I do not understand your American jokes."

"First the sign, then the jokes. You say you don't understand? Well, welcome to the Home of the Free. But remember, also the *Land of the Brave*." And they stood there, Cal finally having the last word, until two cop cars pulled up.

3

THE ADRENALINE RUSH THAT had surged through Cal's body was waning now, leaving a frighteningly empty void. The only good thing was that she found a parking spot right in front of the building the P. F. Underhill Company called home. Then again there weren't many people rushing to work at seven-thirty on a Friday night. She grabbed her camcorder in case Fred wanted to relive the good part of her day.

The firm was incognito in the building directory, the way a good PI usually preferred to be. As she climbed the stairs to the second floor, Cal was met by a thin-bordering-on-bony woman running down.

"Linda! Why are you still here?" Cal said to the firm's secretary.

"Cal, ohmygod, are you all right? Fred told me about the accident. I didn't want to leave until you got here."

"I'll live. Don't worry," said Cal, fighting a sudden wave of dizziness.

Linda kept up her questions as they went up the stairs. "How bad was it? Did you go to the hospital? I thought I heard sirens."

"I'm okay. I'm okay," Cal didn't want to talk in the stairwell. The high-strung secretary was wound up and jittery even on an ordinary day. Linda stopped her at the first landing and wouldn't let her continue up the stairs.

"I got rear-ended near Van Ness. The company van's still driveable. I'm not hurt at all," Cal said, feeling her neck locking up stiffly. There was no way she'd admit to being hurt on the job. She hated claims in all shapes and forms, especially her own. She investigated them; she didn't have them.

"Let me check your pupils," Linda said, peering into Cal's eyes.

"No, Linda, that's for a concussion." As irritating as she could be, Cal sometimes felt that the secretary was a truly genuine person and cared about her. There weren't that many people she felt cared at all. "I appreciate your concern, Linda, I really do."

"Well, look, I gotta go. I want to get home before it's dark. I just wanted to make sure you could walk." Linda looked positively bug-eyed in the dim light.

"It's dark outside now," Cal said.

"Oh, Jesus. Cal, look, this is for you. I hope you won't be too injured to use it." Linda thrust a brown-wrapped package at her.

Cal mumbled a quick thank-you, her mind still focused on the accident.

"You know I worry about you. And that last case—by the skin of your teeth you got out of that one. I typed the final report. I oughta know!" Linda followed Cal as she began again to trek up the stairs. "I oughta know," she repeated. Cal smelled cigarette smoke puff over in a nauseating whiff. "Did you write back and get a refill on your self-defense spray?" Linda probed like the very investigators she typed for, a hundred and ten words a minute at that.

"Refill?"

"It's in the guarantee," Linda explained as if it were gospel. "You use your spray in an attack and they refill it—for free!"

Cal felt relief mixed with apprehension as they reached the office door. She didn't want to deal with Fred and his agenda. "How very kind of them," she responded to Linda. "I didn't, but I'll look for the address. And now—"

Linda sprang in front of Cal as she reached for the doorknob and threw her skinny arm out like a parking gate. "Wait!" she choked out.

"What—? Look, Linda. I don't mean to be abrupt with you but this just isn't the time. I don't have the—"

"There's someone in there with Fred." The secretary struggled to explain.

"Linda—" Cal grasped her arm gently. "You go on home now. I mean it. I'll wait for Fred, okay?" Cal opened the door and they both went inside the office.

"I wanted to warn you," Linda whispered, and grabbed her purse from the drawer where she kept it. "You take care now, you hear? I'm glad you're okay. I care—I care about you, Cal." Linda hugged her, but Cal, when she felt herself pulled forward, felt her neck lock up even more. It was an extremely unpleasant sensation. Linda left, taking one million frenetic ions with her.

Cal knocked on Fred's door, something she never did. But through all the gibberish Linda had spouted came the one word—"warn." There was no answer. What was going on? She knocked again. Who was in there with Fred? Who, what, where, and when? Silence. And don't forget the why.

"Fred. Fred," she called out, her imagination for once totally bereft.

"Just wait," came a terse reply.

As far as she knew, Fred was happily married so she didn't really think he was carrying on with some woman in there, although these days there wasn't much you could be certain of. Also, he didn't have a couch and his desk wasn't that big. She tried to shake her head as she made her way back toward her own office but her neck wouldn't let it happen.

Without Linda's presence the rooms were eerily calm. That is, until she rounded the corner and ran smack into Steve Orella.

"What are you doing in San Francisco?" she blurted, and then was instantly abashed. He was an investigator in the southern California office. "Oh, I'm sorry. I didn't mean—"

She thought Orella peered at her as if she were an insect under glass. She had no idea he was so nervous around her that he ceased functioning under his own impulse, going instead on autopilot; she put him into twitch mode.

"You. Okay?" The words came out as if they were being

squeezed out of a toothpaste tube. He was as tongue-tied as a schoolboy with his first crush.

"Fine. Couldn't be better. Jim-dandy." Cal hated men who attracted her and were exactly her type. Black shagged hair with electric green eyes. Physiques that made her think of darkened rooms and private moments. A real possibility for a long-term relationship. Orella. One of the enemy, to be sure. She had despised Orella on sight from the very first minute she had met him at a computer training session in Glendale.

Her usage of the term jim-dandy was also unfortunate; it zoomed at warp speed through her train of thought, leaving a trail of distracted memories in its wake. Her last case, involving a Jim, had nearly been her undoing, both personally and professionally. More randy than dandy.

"Why are you holding your neck like that?" Orella asked.

Cal wanted to spit a none-of-your-business at him, but this wasn't family. This was work. And staying in Orella's good graces was necessary since he was a hell-raiser in the research department.

"I'm not holding my neck like anything," Cal denied.

"It's freezing up on you, isn't it? I had a whipper myself, couple of years ago." Orella's eyes held her like a voodoo spell. "You should get it looked at," he cautioned in a softer tone. They had often worked together via telephone, which taught him to tread carefully when giving Cal advice.

There was silence as they both thought the same thing: how each had sounded on the phone that time Cal had called on a case at two in the morning.

Cal recovered first. "I am not going to, even if it is hurt. I don't want to fill out a worker comp claim form. I don't want to go into the damn index system." Cal touched her neck. "Shit," she said.

"You never swear," Orella reminded her. "Remember how you explained to me you worked around too many men to let yourself fall into that habit?"

"Too many ex-cops. And 'shit' is not swearing, dammit. Darn index system." Cal was getting irritated. What she could swear was that her back was getting numb.

"It could get worse," he said.

"How?"

"You could have popped a disc."

"Damn. Damn. Damn that sixteen-year-old. And most likely he's unlicensed, uninsured, and an illegal alien to boot."

"If you go to the doctor, just don't tell him you were working," suggested Orella.

"I've seen the forms come in that the health insurance carriers make you complete. It would come out sooner or later. Besides, I'm a fraud investigator—we're not supposed to lie."

Orella made sympathetic noises. Cal wished he would turn annoying and chiding again; she could deal with him better on those terms.

"You here to sightsee?" She tried a new tack. What if, she suddenly panicked, he was here to replace her? It was a good time to think such thoughts, taking her mind off her brand-new aches and pains and future medical possibilities.

The business world held its own brand of nightmare. Anything was possible there as well.

"Nah, business."

"A case?" Cal wouldn't let it go.

"I think I better let Fred tell you."

Cal wanted to react but she didn't want Orella to see how this affected her. "I knocked on his door but he told me to wait."

"He was tied up."

Cal could have said something. Maybe the old Cal would have. But the new Cal only stared.

"You're doing that again," Orella said, "with your neck."

"I'll live."

Orella and Cal sat side by side in front of Fred Underhill's desk like schoolchildren being reprimanded by the principal. Fred's thick black eyebrows were drawn downward, as were the corners of his mouth. Also the glimmer of a joke about to be told that usually danced in his eyes was absent. Not a good sign.

He wouldn't look this way if it was only me getting fired, Cal reasoned. *And Orella wouldn't be in here. Something's up. Something big.*

"Doesn't feel like a Friday." Cal tried to warm up the chill in the room. "More like a Monday. Not good, a Friday feeling like a Monday. In fact, I can't recall a—"

"Cal, I've got some news," Fred cut her off.

"News to me, I mean, for me?"

"I've got some . . . bad news."

"Why was Steve told first, why—" she said, her words rushing out.

"The company's been sold," Fred blurted.

"Sold," Cal echoed. She looked first at Fred, then to Orella. A chill ran up and down her spine. Her arms tingled. Her whiplash, finally, was forgotten as it all went south. They all looked at each other for a long moment as no one spoke.

"Who?" said Cal. She was glad the word was one syllable, two could possibly have cracked.

"Worldwide Investigations," said Fred.

"How wide?" Cal was dazed and confused but attempting to keep her sense of humor.

"Worldwide," Fred hoarsely whispered.

"Gee," said Cal.

Orella did not speak. He looked at a distant spot on the wall. Then he seemed fascinated by his shoe.

"Steve has been transferred here. They're bringing in their own people for southern California. And I'm—I'm going out on my own," Fred said. "There's language in the contract P. F. entered into about not soliciting or working for current clients."

Cal didn't move, not even to blink. She waited for him to speak again. For once, being the owner's nephew hadn't been an asset for Fred.

"You'll be going with the new company," he said after a long pause. The acne scars on his rugged face looked like craters.

"This reminds me of a slave auction," Cal said, the usual tone coming into her voice for the first time. "Sold to the highest bidder. P. F. sold out. I had no idea."

"They told me your first assignment for the new company will get you on the road. Reno."

"Reno," Cal responded dully.

"There'll be a Worldwide supervisor here Monday," said Fred.

"Steve didn't get the position," Cal said.

"Worldwide has their own management staff."

"I bet."

"Cal," warned Fred.

"I fled the totalitarian regime when I left Summit," Cal said. "Working here was a step in my work release program."

"Give it a chance, Cal," said Fred.

"Leaves me no choice," she responded. "Gotta pay the rent. The bills."

"By the bye, how are you?" Fred asked. "You hurt?"

"Only my pride," Cal said. "But wait till you see the van. That pretty picture will help get me off on the right foot with the new top brass."

"Oh, they'll be entranced with our resident bad girl." Fred smiled for the first time.

"Fred, bad things happen to bad girls. I think the passenger's going to sue me." Cal tried not to rub her neck.

"Don't be silly. He's in the wrong car."

"I've seen people sue in stranger circumstances. You know, Fred. You've seen them sue when there's no damage to either car. Maybe they're in a Russian ring and it was a set up."

"They would have been in front of you, Cal."

"I think that's what they were trying to do. Only problem was, they were in too much of a rush to get there!"

Somehow it worked out that Orella was driving Cal home. Fred promised to have someone bring the Firebird out to her place in the morning. His last official act as head of the office, Cal realized sadly. She felt drained, exhausted, and didn't protest much about the lift to North Beach.

Orella's ride was a pristine, gleaming black Corvette. Cal wondered if she'd be able to get herself into the low-slung car. Then she wondered if she'd need a forklift to get back out.

Orella didn't have much to say as they drove toward Cal's apartment on Green street. San Francisco was on display wearing her bright lights. The city filled with Friday-night energy. Cal, however, only wanted to sleep. But she felt she should be polite.

"How do you think you're going to like living here?" she asked him. "After L.A., I mean." She had never been alone with Orella before.

"Well, it's so sudden. Such a fast change. I hate moving. Have to get a place. Get Mighty Dog up here."

Cal stifled a yawn. "He'll be okay. I can picture him on these hills."

"One fire hydrant's just like another to him."

"Is it to you? I mean, do you know anyone here in the city?"

"Not a soul."

"Are you implying I'm no one?" Cal teased.

"Don't want to burden you. I'll get by." Orella was being stoic.

"I was born here. Know this place like the back of my hand. You need to know anything, just ask. I'll show you around."

"Thanks, Cal. I really appreciate that," Orella looked at her out of the corner of his eye. "Sure is beautiful. The city," he stammered.

"It's home. And I'm sure you'll be all right here. The earthquakes are right on a par with L.A."

"Why bring up natural disasters? Did you ever notice you look for the worst in everything?" Orella said.

"I always thought I looked for the best." Cal was wounded. "That earthquake crack—I just meant it as a joke." Cal wished she was at home already. Alone. Away from Orella's sexy stare. The last, totally, absolutely last thing she wanted was to get involved with someone. Let alone someone in a work situation.

It was one of the Brantley commandments.

First, there had been a disastrous teenage romance with a local boy. Sexual awakening, her mother, who was into Tantric teachings, called it.

Then she had met David Brantley, dropped out of college, and married him, a month short of her nineteenth birthday. Marriage apparently hadn't agreed with David: one night he went out for cigarettes and never returned.

What befell him was a mystery, but in Cal's heart she felt she knew the answer—he had escaped from their life together. In a way unsettled, unfinished business, but she had chalked it up to a failure on her own part.

Humiliated, she fled San Francisco, traveling as far cross-country as she could get from friends and family. Away from anyone who knew what had happened. In Miami, she got a job as an adjuster with Summit Insurance Company, first working a desk and then promoted to the field.

At Summit, she had met a co-worker, Michael, and fallen in love. Michael's wife had left him for another man, and Cal thought they had a lot in common. But relationships born of stormy endings sometimes have their own rocky conclusion, and theirs was the rule, rather than the exception. The breakup tore Cal's life asunder, both personally and professionally. Never date anyone at the local water cooler.

And so she had run again, run for her life—back home, hoping people would forget her incredibly bad batting average. She had, in her own mind, struck out.

"No," Orella was saying, "you're a black-and-white person."

"Better than your everyday gray," she snapped back. "Look, Steve, I can get out here."

"I don't know a lot about this place but I don't think this is North Beach. Or even close."

"I feel like walking. I do."

"That makes sense. C'mon, after your car accident you feel like a stroll. I think you're going to have some problems with these hills. I'll take you home."

"A take-charge man." Cal was getting irritated in spite of herself.

"You don't like men much, do you?"

"Let's not get off on tangents," Cal warned. "Not if we're going to be working together. Closely. Working closely together." *Shut up, Cal. Shut up,* she warned herself.

"You know, you've got a chip the size of Gibraltar." He was getting steamed.

"I thought you were giving me a ride, not psychoanalyzing me." Cal's voice rose.

"Hey. Calm down. Peace. Pax. Okay. Maybe you're a little shook up."

"Maybe more than a little. You think it's fun getting smacked at forty-five miles an hour by some twerp?"

"Which irks you more, the company being sold or the accident and the twerp?" Orella was glad they were on a new subject.

"The twerp, to be sure. All the accidents I've investigated. Now I'm in one. My first! Now I guess I'll have greater insight. A new training course for investigators." Cal sighed. "And the new company. No way can I start with a work comp claim right off the bat. This job can really be miserable when the higher-ups cop an attitude."

"I'm glad you're not hurt worse." Orella let it slip.

Cal was still seething from the black-and-white remark; she hardly noticed. "Now you're going to be working up here. *Quelle change.*"

"Worldwide doesn't do asset checks. That's not their cup

of tea. Or backgrounds. I'll be out in the field. Maybe we'll get to work a case or two together."

"You were very helpful to me on that last case, Steve," Cal said, deciding to toss him a compliment—see what happened.

"Lots of research on that one. You didn't know the half of it."

"It was a good job."

"You cracked the case, Cal." He was now in her corner.

"Hang a right here."

"Whoa! Up the hill."

"Up the hill."

"This is what I call a real hill."

"Keeps out the fainthearted."

Steve gave the car some gas. "C'mon, Growly."

"Growly?"

"My car."

Look out, San Francisco. Here comes Mr. Steve, Mighty Dog, and Growly. Cal spotted the red geraniums in the window boxes of her third-floor apartment. She recalled the day she had planted those in the spring. The air, so clear, tinged with the promise of the season, the day—her day, so quiet, still, each moment wrapped in the clarity of soil, planting, introspection. A day too still in memory. A day all to herself, all by herself.

"That's my place there, with the red flowers," she said, pointing it out to Orella.

. . .

He insisted on coming upstairs; he wanted to see his first San Francisco habitat. Cal had resisted.

"I worry about your car," she protested weakly. "Growly, parked out on the street here." She appealed to Orella's fastidious side. "People have a tendency to nudge cars when they pull in and out of parking spots. Most of the cars you see in the city are clunkers."

"They nudge in L.A. too. I won't stay long." He was determined, she could see that.

"C'mon, then."

He followed her up the three flights of stairs. She tried not to wince, but when they got to her door and she dropped the keys, he was the one who kneeled to retrieve them. Her pain was increasing but denial of its existence had become an unspoken pact between them.

"What a view!" Orella exclaimed as he looked out at the sparkling lights.

"That's the Transamerica Pyramid." Cal showed him, aware that they were standing very close to each other. "See, it's a big triangle."

"Yeah," whispered Orella, his shyness returning.

"Hello. Anybody home?" a woman's voice called out from the doorway. Cal and Orella jumped apart, startled.

"Doesn't anybody knock around here?" Cal said to the interloper.

"Knocking's for strangers, we're almost kin. Besides, I've told you, lock the door!"

"My neighbor from the first floor, Laurie Stern." Cal

made the introductions. "Steve Orella." Cal made the statements short, hoping Laurie would get the hint. Laurie was wearing her usual slathered-on heavy eye makeup, but it didn't help cover up the once-over she was giving Orella.

"Steve works at P. F. Underhill," Cal said. "Actually, as of today, Worldwide. He gave me a lift home." One more hint, a bigger one.

"Oh, did your Firebird break down?" Laurie made herself comfortable on the sofa. Once she heard Orella wasn't a date she switched gears, unfortunately they were the wrong ones.

"I wonder how many times I'm going to have to tell this story," Cal said wearily to Orella.

"We could write it on a piece of cardboard and you could hold it up," Steve offered.

"That could very well be in my future."

"You've lost me," Laurie said.

Cal gave her a look that said "I wish."

"You know, Cal, you look like you've been in a train wreck."

"How kind of you to notice, Laurie. If all my friends were as considerate as you, I wouldn't need enemies."

"We're best friends," Laurie said to Orella, giving him a twice-over.

"Has anyone ever told you—" Orella started to say.

"—that she looks just like—" Cal cut in.

"Janis Joplin?" Laurie finished.

"Incredible," Orella said, looking at Laurie with greater interest.

"Can't take her anywhere," said Cal. "People are always

coming up to us. I've threatened her with telling them she's really Janis's illegitimate daughter."

"Is she?" Orella asked.

Laurie cackled like Janis. "Well, Cal. I'm here. Have you forgotten? We were on for tonight. Pasta. You promised."

Cal held the side of her face with one hand. "I forgot, Laur. I'm sorry. What with the car accident and the company being sold—it's been a bit too much."

"Whoa—what car accident? Are you okay?"

"Clipped me on the left rear fender. Forty-five miles an hour. Sixteen-year-old uninsured illegal alien."

"You've got it down, Cal," Orella tried to make her smile. "In your black-and-white style."

Cal gave him a pained expression, then turned to Laurie. "I hate to say it, Laur. But I'm not up to cooking."

"Then let's go out. You need to eat."

Orella was looking at them with a pitiful expression. Cal wondered if Mighty Dog had a doleful look to match his master's.

"Steve. I'm sorry. I did promise Laurie." There was no nice way to ask him to leave.

Again that look, but Cal kept firm. No more green-eyed men in her future, especially ones she worked with. Steve looked as if he didn't have a friend in the world. He turned toward the door.

"Steve, wait. I'll tell you what. Are you still going to be in town tomorrow night?"

"I can hang around. Start my search for a new apartment."

"Good. My aunt Sue and uncle Nick are having a big celebration for their twenty-fifth anniversary. It's at eight o'clock. You can come with me. Protect me from my seven cousins. When I was a kid they took turns beating me up."

"Made you tough," Laurie called out.

"That explains it," Orella said.

Cal opened the door, not feeling so bad about hustling him out. She wanted them to be friends. Work friends.

"Take care of yourself," he cautioned Cal. "Nice meeting you, Laurie. See if you can get her to rest."

"I'm going to see if I can find any muscle relaxers left over from my car accident." Laurie had gotten up and joined them at the door. "Nothing like two of those babies."

"It'll mix nicely with the wine tomorrow night. Pick me up at seven-thirty? The party's in Berkeley."

"Seven-thirty it is. And Cal—you really shouldn't mix pills with booze."

"I was just joking. I never take any kind of medicine. I have to be absolutely crawling to even take a Tylenol."

Orella left, waving to both Laurie and Cal at the door. Why did Cal get the feeling three was a crowd? From the street she could hear Growly start up, and not so far away, a cable car bell clanged. Was it a warning sound—was she letting Orella get too close? Or perhaps the notes were cheerful?

"You know, Ms. Stern, I don't think I'm up to pasta in any form tonight. Even if I'm not cooking, it seems like too much trouble. It would be nice to have little bite-size pieces of food."

"Chinese?"

"Takeout?"

"You're on," said Laurie.

4

"**WELL, LOOK AT YOU!**" The door swung open to the house on Ashby Street and Cal was immediately in her aunt Sue's arms. Her back spasmed; she had never felt so out of control of her body, except perhaps in a bad love affair.

"Nick, California's here!"

Cal winced, this time at the "California." "I'm eternally grateful they didn't give me a middle name," she said to Steve. "It would have been Sunflower. Or Strawberry Fields—"

"Cal, Cal." She was enveloped in her favorite uncle's arms. "Let me look at you. I guess I can't say how you've grown anymore."

"No, Uncle Nick. I've been done with that for quite a while."

"But ah, *che bella donna!* And as beautiful on the inside as the outside. And who is the lucky man?"

"Steve. Steve Orella. I *work* with Steve, Uncle Nick. He has been transferred to San Francisco."

"From?"

"L.A." Orella spoke for the first time. "I'm pleased to meet you both." He shook hands with Nick and then Sue.

"Remember—never call it Frisco," Sue said. "It's a dead giveaway. And maybe"—here she dropped her voice—"it's best if you don't tell anybody about the L.A. part."

"Oh, Aunt Sue!" Cal laughed.

Sue closed the front door and they made their way toward the boisterous crowd. "He'll have to decompress up here in the cleaner air."

"Like scuba-diving," Nick added.

"They double-teamed me the entire time I was growing up. The normal kind of life I failed to get from my own parents, I tried to get here."

"Has anyone ever done a study of how the kids of flower children turn out?" A girl in her early twenties with thick blond, almost kinky hair came up to Cal and hugged her.

"Gigi!" Cal exclaimed, hugging her in return and remembering instantaneously the previous day's accident; it was repeating on her like a spicy burrito. "It's been so long."

"Too long, cuz. Where you been keeping yourself?"

Cal thought of just how much willpower it had taken her to come to this party. Inwardly she cringed at the thought of someone bringing up her past, even peripherally.

"Steve, I want you to meet my cousin Gianna. We were like sisters growing up." Cal suddenly looked wistful, a new expression flitting across her face, one that Orella had not caught a glimpse of until that moment.

"Gigi, what's happening? What are you up to?"

"I've rebelled, in my own way, by going straight." Gigi grinned and in that grin Orella saw a strong family resemblance. "Kids of the hippies," Gigi explained to Orella, "have no qualms about making money. Up until I was ten, I had this fantasy about my mom in an apron and my dad going to work, a regular necktie dad."

"Gigi was born when they lived at a commune," Cal added.

"Actually I was born in a garden there, where my parents followed the Chicago Policemen's Handbook to Childbirthing. It's a miracle I don't have brain damage."

"My mom would try with my straight friends," Cal said. "But to this day I still feel like I have to cover for her partying."

"Man, I still have to take a good sniff when I come here, just to make sure the coast is clear." Gigi winked at Orella.

"But at least you know what kinds of presents will make the biggest hit," Cal said. "This is for you, Uncle Nick and Aunt Sue." She handed over a square box Orella had been holding. "Happy anniversary."

Sue ripped the gift wrap and opened the box. "Oh, Cal. A lava light!"

"Just like the one I broke when I was six."

"We love it. Thank you," exclaimed Sue. "I want to plug it in, I'll be right back."

"Play your song, Mom. You know, the Rare Earth thing," Gigi said as her mother turned away with the lamp. "At least they're not lame parents," Gigi said, "they're cool." Minutes later, the stereo came on.

"So, Gigi, what are you up to? You never did say," Cal asked.

"Oh, I'm working for Benny." Gianna turned around and showed Cal and Orella the back of her T-shirt, which read, Marin Bail Bonds, Est. 1989. "I heard you're a real PI."

"As opposed to a fake PI," said Cal. If she tried to get everyone in a really great mood, maybe it would help her forget about her neck and back. "I'm sorry, you must be bored," she said to Orella. "Dragging you to this reunion."

"Crank it, Mom," yelled Gianna. The stereo went up a notch. Sue reappeared to join them.

"This is fine," responded Orella. "I'm glad I came."

"I like your new boyfriend, Cal," Sue said.

"Stop teasing, Aunt Sue. I told you, he's someone I work with." Sue always was good at pushing Cal's buttons and it seemed as though start was being pressed. Cal's aunt ran a New Age bookstore on Telegraph Avenue and had absorbed the self-help literature like a sponge, homing in on what made people tick.

"What was that old expression, Aunt Sue? 'You're giving me bad vibes,' " Cal said.

"You're talking the talk, girl," said Sue. "But work, play, it doesn't matter where you meet a good man."

"And you know what they say—" Gianna said, but Cal cut her off.

"Behave! You do skip traces and stuff like that?" Cal said, anxious to change the subject.

"Yeah." Gianna was temporarily diverted. "We hunt down the bad guys. All of the ones that jump bail are usually *really* bad. I never meet anyone through work. But it's not like what you do, Cal. Or is it?"

"Well, I do have to say we are also occasionally exposed to the lower elements of society."

"Are you a PI too?" Nick asked Orella. Nick had been quietly taking the measure of the man and liking what he saw.

"Well, yes. But right now I'm working under the company license."

"The company's been sold, Uncle Nick. It's Worldwide Investigations now, not P. F. Underhill," said Cal.

"With clients all over the place," offered Steve.

"They'll probably send me to Kansas," said Cal glumly.

"Dorothy liked it," said Gianna.

"Is my dad here yet?" Cal asked.

"Not yet," said Sue, "but we're hoping he can make it. You know he hates these family things."

"He hates families, period," said Cal. "Where are the drinks?" she said abruptly. "I'm thirsty. Steve, how about you?"

"C'mon. Let's get you fixed up." Nick led them over to a long table where the drinks were. "There's wine."

"There's always wine. Any of those Italian sodas from Molinari's? I could go for one of those."

"Have you ever been to a party here when we didn't have Italian sodas?" Nick handed her a full glass. Orella poured himself a red wine.

"Never been much for that side of the Italian psyche," said Cal, referring to the wine. "Makes me feel a bit guilty though," she added as she sipped her soda. "An Italian who doesn't like wine."

"Maybe your Jewish side is kicking in," said Gianna. "But guilt—you? I don't buy it, Cal. Even as a kid I recall that once you made up your mind to do something, no matter how risky, for you there was no looking back."

"Well, happy anniversary, Uncle and Aunt. Now"—she turned to Orella—"let's eat!"

"What did she mean by 'your Jewish side'?" asked Steve as they made for the table laden with food.

"I'm a mutt," Cal said. "My Mom's Jewish. Dad's Italian. They separated when I was a baby, but never divorced. Here, try some of this. Zucchini lasagna, my aunt's specialty."

"Are they vegetarians?"

"Big-time. No red meat, and don't get them started, especially Sue. Tell her you eat meat and she'll try to convert you. She says that if she stops just one person from eating animals, she'll have saved a certain number; she has the whole thing calculated out."

"My folks are different. Very materialistic," Steve said between bites.

Cal gave a short laugh. "Uncle Nick was a mime at Fisherman's Wharf for a long time. Then he did sketches of the tourists."

"They're not what I expected," said Orella.

"Just remember, as a rule, no one is what you expect," said Cal seriously.

"I'm really glad you asked me to this party, Cal." Orella looked as serious as Cal now. "This company shake-up—

well-it's shaken me up. I'm not really going with the flow, as your aunt and uncle would put it."

"Let's eat, drink, and be merry, for tomorrow, who knows. Maybe we'll both be out on the street," said Cal.

"Your cheerfulness is overwhelming."

"You heard what they said about me. Even as a child I was ruthless. But it's true, you know. We could be without a job. Maybe Worldwide will be bringing their own people in."

"As I understand it, we're part of the deal. Just management is Worldwide."

"Why do I hate that word management?"

"Sounds like the thread of nonconformity that runs through your clan hasn't missed you," Steve offered. "Maybe someday you'll go out on your own. When you have enough hours you'll get your license. Start your own agency."

"Someday," Cal said simply.

"And I don't have contacts. No clients."

"Soon we'll be in the field together," said Cal. "The disenfranchised and unlicensed."

"You're a kick. A regular bulldozer," said Orella.

"Roll right over everyone and everything in my path," said Cal.

"Even your own team?"

"Men think of everything in sports terms," said Cal bluntly.

"They do?" Orella gulped his wine. "I think that at some level you should be glad Worldwide is attempting to make this a smooth transition. Try to look at it as a positive, not a negative."

"It's just so sudden," Cal said.

"But isn't that what you enjoy about this business? Change. Diversity. Every day a new mix. You've got to admit, this job's never tedious. And next week, you'll be in Reno."

"Oh, yeah, the new case Fred mentioned for me in Reno." Cal tried to sound enthusiastic but Orella saw she wasn't smiling.

"I'd like to meet your dad," said Orella.

"So would I," said Cal.

"I'd say you've got yourself a pistol," said a stocky man standing close to Cal's elbow. She turned, startled. "Tony!" she exclaimed, putting her plate down. She wondered how long he had been there. He regarded them both with sleepy, hooded eyes that were a brilliant aquamarine color and bloodshot.

Cal glanced at the door as if she wanted to check out the escape route. "What a surprise."

"Cal's my best girl," he slurred to Orella. "Is she your best girl?"

"Tony, this is Steve Orella—Tony Lazio. I work with Steve, Tony. Not that I owe you an explanation."

"While you're at it, why don't you go on and tell Steve here how you're my best girl."

"Was, Tony, was. Long, long ago." She turned to Orella. "Tony and I were an item ten years ago."

"Has it been that long? Seems to me that only a couple

of months ago, we were close to gettin' it on. Remember, Cal? Pelican Bay, or have you got one of those selective memories?" Tony took a packet of purple-colored mints out of his pocket and popped one in his mouth. There was a strong scent of lavender.

"You're the one with early onset dementia." Cal's eyes held a nasty glint.

"Cal, Cal. Always with the tender compliments. You can see how she's really crazy about me."

Cal shook her head in disgust. "Tony, you're drunk. Or is your current state drug induced?"

"You're wrong, wrong, wrong. What you're observing is a medical condition."

"Sure—it's called stoned," said Cal without any sympathy.

"You work with Mr. Steve here, huh? Have you told him how I am indispensable on your little investigative forays?"

"Yeah, right," said Cal.

"The dog, remember the dog," said Tony.

"Okay, so you came in handy."

"Now, Steve. You can listen up here and get some real insight into how the female mind works. We show up a little uninvited and we're brutes. We save their nice little butts, we come in handy. Open your ears Steve, my boy. Listen to what your intended is saying. Soon you'll be nothing more than a Handi Wipe."

"Tony!" Cal admonished. "You're wiped out! I told you, we work together."

"Who works under who?" Tony's face was getting beet

red and streaks of sweat ran down from his temples to his chin.

"Okay, man," Orella said. "You've had enough of whatever it is you're partaking of—I've had enough of you." Orella's face was grim. Cal was startled; she was seeing another side to Orella, one that she thought she'd better file away for further reflection.

The two men stood face-to-face, squaring off, although Tony was several inches shorter than Orella.

"Problem here?" A huge man had walked up to the ugly little scene. The newcomer was about five ten and two hundred eighty pounds. Every pound was tight muscle, every movement rippled menace. Orella saw a strong resemblance to Cal in the man's features.

"Cousin Benny!"

"Callie, how you been?" He reached forward as if to hug her. Gianna, by his side, winked at Orella.

Cal stepped back. "Not so great, Benny. I'm afraid I have to pass on the hug. I was in a car accident yesterday. Clobbered by—" Here she paused as if cranking up for a long-winded explanation.

"A sixteen-year-old unlicensed, uninsured illegal alien," Orella finished for her.

"Do you think we could make it a song, like that teeny weeny yellow polka-dot bikini?" said Cal, overly glad that Benny's presence and the loopy turn of the conversation had headed off a confrontation at the OK Corral.

"Gotta give my favorite cuz a kiss, though," said Benny, kissing Cal on the forehead.

"Kissin' cousins. Steve needs to know everything about the wild Donadio side of your psyche," said Gianna. "For future reference."

"Gigi, Steve is just a colleague," Cal said, starting to wonder herself.

"Methinks the lady doth protest too much," said Gianna.

"See—" Tony was cranking up again.

"Tony, c'mere, buddy," Benny put a massive arm around Tony, who was suddenly dwarfed by the much larger man. "Let's take a short quiz, my main man." Benny turned slightly and his Marin Bail Bond shirt looked like an advertisement on the back of a bus bench.

"Hummph," gurgled Tony in Benny's embrace.

"Now, first question—" Everyone got in closer to hear the exchange. "What is today?" said Benny softly.

"Saturday," replied Tony obediently.

"No, dude. C'mon. Now, take it from the top and think, my man, think. What is today?"

Tony's face went from red to white. Cal knew from Benny's brotherly kiss that his breath was a blast of garlic and onions. Tony, however, didn't flinch; Cal had to hand that to him.

"Today," Benny told him, "is my parents' twenty-fifth anniversary. A day which, any normal person knows, comes only once.

"Now. Second question. Why are you here?"

"Because I know everyone here and—" Benny was nodding encouragingly. "And my folks are friends their whole lives with your folks. And we grew up together." Tony finished like a schoolchild who up until that very minute had been the class dunce, but had finally managed to get one fact right in the past five years.

"Better. Better. Now, third and final question. What will happen if you ruin this happy party for my mom and dad and cousin Cal and her guest here?"

"You'll beat the crap out of me, Benny, just like you did the entire time we were growing up."

"Bingo! You win. That and three dollars will get you across the Golden Gate Bridge. You may now proceed with your life." Benny let go of Tony and gave him a little push.

"But can't you see, Benny?" Tony's eyes opened wider and his face went paler. "Can't you all see? I've got no life. I'm a total screwup. Losing Cal started it. And then it snowballed into something bigger and bigger. And then there's the accident, making it a hundred an' twenny percent. Maybe, yeah, maybe more than that. It's all fucked. An' I'm all fucked up. Totally. And do you realize, hell, I've realized, that there's no—absolutely no—going back?"

"Hey, man, lighten up," said Benny, alarmed at this outburst.

"Yeah. You're starting to sound like a Doobie Brothers song." Cal said.

"My life is over," said Tony, and maneuvering somewhat shakily around clusters of people, walked out the front door.

"Poor slob," Benny said, shaking his head.

"What a drag," Gianna said.

"No, no. That guy's in serious shape," said Cal.

"No shit," said Benny. "C'mon. Let's party, man." He

turned to Steve. "You dating my best cuz, I need to show you around. Make some intros to the people."

"Benny, he's not—" Cal started to say as Benny led Steve away. "Oh, what the hell," she said to Gianna, "I'll never convince any of you."

"When you wish upon a star, little black sheep. Best advice I could give," said Gianna.

"There, finally!" said Cal.

"Finally what?"

"Finally someone has come right out and said it."

"Said what? Spit it out."

"I am the black sheep of this family."

"Cuz, for this family, that's the ultimate honor," said Gianna. "You're the head renegade. No one has ever understood you. Now, let's party hearty. And want to know a secret? My mom and dad stayed together this long just so they could say they were together this long."

"That makes absolutely no sense," said Cal, "but somehow I see your point. Lead me to the wine. I think, after all, I will have that drink."

"Make it a few. Try living down to your reputation for a change."

5

MONDAY MORNING.

Orella back in L.A. (not for long) and Cal in her sweats, doing her thing. Stretches, breakfast, a walk in the direction of the Golden Gate Bridge and back to North Beach. The hills of San Francisco would either prolong her life or kill her. This morning it was torture.

Usually she did free weights but her neck was so stiff it was not feasible. Walking up an incline sent a piercing pain down into her hip. She rebelled against the thought that total inertia was the only course of action. Mentally and physically she was going to fight this injury. She tossed the muscle relaxers that Laurie had left for her into a drawer.

Cal was getting out of the shower when she heard her pager going off. Paged on a Monday morning—Fred would never stoop so low. But then her heart and spirits took a nosedive with the realization that as of today *there was no Fred.*

She played the Who's vintage album and listened to them

sing "We Won't Be Fooled Again" twice before calling the office.

Linda answered the phone sounding as if she were hyperventilating. "Oh, Cal, Cal. You better get in here. They've been asking where you are."

"I'm a field investigator, Linda. Calm down. I'm out in the field."

"Cal, this is not funny. They're here. She's here. She said to page you and that when you called in you'd better come in. Pronto."

"Tell her I'm working a case."

"It's not going to fly, Cal. I already tried. She wanted to know the case number."

"We don't have numbers."

"I told her. She didn't say anything. Just looked at me and did something weird with her eyebrows. That was the worst part."

"Her eyebrows?"

"No. The way she didn't say anything." Linda's breath made a weird whooshing noise that carried disturbingly from Cal's ear to her brain. Monday morning and Linda was directly in Cal's head.

"Linda, you've got to calm down. You're getting carried away. I'm sure the situation can be resolved without calling out the—" Cal nearly said the National Guard, but stopped herself. With Linda you couldn't get into specifics in a joke. "Look, tell her I worked seventy-five hours last week and I'm—"

"Cal. That's another thing. Your time sheet's back on your desk."

"So?"

"There's a little yellow sticky on it."

"So?"

"You better get in here." Linda's voice rose in pitch.

"Is she young or old or in-between?"

"I can't—I can't talk now, Cal. I think she's taping this." Linda was flipping, Cal thought, maybe she had been around investigators too much. Paranoia sets in. Or—maybe not.

"I'll be in," Cal said simply, and hung up.

A worker in overalls was scraping off the last *L* in Underhill with a razor as Cal trudged up the final stairs. Her neck was locked up so tight she felt her head was tilting to one side.

The workman leered at her as she went inside. She smiled at him in return; possibly she'd be back in a few minutes in order to ask if she could borrow his razor.

"Go in right away." Linda's face was positively ochre.

"*Merci beaucoup,*" Cal replied. She'd make a concerted effort to respond with joy to each miserable thing that came her way. "Monday, Monday, can't trust that day," sang the Mamas and Papas. With good reason, Cal thought. She'd handle this—she wouldn't let the neck pain, the sixteen-year-old driver, the man with the razor, or even what awaited her behind the green door spoil her damn day. Slipping, slipping. *Her* day, not her *damn* day.

A woman in her late forties sat behind Fred's desk. Cal read the shiny brass nameplate—DeMille. The woman's hair was dyed a dull jet black and pulled back in a tight bun. As Cal entered the room, the woman bared all her teeth in what Cal supposed was a supervisor's version of a smile.

Like jungle animals marking their own territories, they introduced themselves. Sixties songs whizzed in and out of Cal's thoughts like Ping-Pong balls. She tried to keep her gaze upward, but her eyes shifted of their own will to the spot where her new boss's dress plunged, her matronly bosom puffing out of her décolletage. A gold cross dangled between the swells.

"Ms. Brantley," she said with a lot of teeth.

"You can call me Cal."

"I'm Carmen DeMille. You can call me Carmen. Nice of you to make it in."

"I'm usually out in the field, Miss Deville."

"DeMille."

"Sorry. Miss DeMille. I rarely come into the office."

"Well, thank you for gracing us with one of your rare appearances."

"I can't bill much in the office."

"For thirty years, I was outside. In the field. There isn't anything I haven't seen. I've done it all. I know every trick in the book. From fraud to arson and back again. I've talked with con men, criminals, psychopaths, child molesters. I've climbed roofs, dug ditches, suited up for dives. I've jumped out of planes, outrun trains." Carmen's eyes were lit by a self-righteous fire; Cal fought against taking a step back. "I've been chased, attacked, shot at, and maimed. I've been spit on and stomped." Here she stopped and took a deep breath. Her visible bosom expanded out of the confines of her experienced undergarments and rose into view even more.

"So don't talk to me about the field. And don't try to scam me with billing. I've got your number and more!"

Cal fought the extreme urge to tell her she hadn't taken a number, but recalled her meager bank balance. She shuffled her feet instead, and found she needed to go to the bathroom.

"I've seen the van," Carmen said in a rather quick leap.

"Yes, the van." Cal heard Linda explode into a coughing fit on the other side of the door.

"There's a lot of damage there."

"I was hit pretty hard."

"Were you in pursuit?"

"No, I had broken off."

"L.A. said you had broken off Thursday."

"Well, you see, I had this feeling. Experienced as you are, you would understand, of course."

"Try me."

Cal thought of her car insurance, electric bill, her charge account; she tried very hard. "Well, you see, I got this hinky feeling sitting on this woman's house. And I thought I should try it one more day. On my own."

"On. Your. Own." Carmen stared at her like a tiger about to devour its prey. "Do you always have a tendency, Ms. Brantley, not to follow directions?"

This was a trick question. "No, I'm good at following

directions." Cal smiled. The monster smiled back. "I just thought it would be best to go ahead and do it." Damn, she had her trapped. In a corner, all the way in.

"Why?"

"Just a hinky feeling . . ."

"We run a tight ship here, young woman." DeMille looked like someone who had just taken a strong laxative. "You will, in the future, follow all of my directives. You will not go off, half-cocked, on your own merry way. I expect you to respond within five minutes of a page. This morning was unacceptable."

"I was in the shower."

"Do that on your own time." Carmen paused. "Linda said you were in the field."

"I was. But I took the shower first. What if I'm driving in heavy traffic?"

"Pardon?"

"You know. Do I have to answer within five minutes if I'm in heavy traffic? It's unsafe to talk on a cell phone—"

"Pull over."

"In an unsafe area?"

"Now." Here Carmen walked around the desk until she was three inches from Cal and staring directly into her eyes. "We need to get on the same level. So there will be no misunderstanding." Cal noticed then that Carmen was shorter than she was; that was a good sign. Did she mean, however, that at this point Cal should kneel?

"Within five minutes, I don't care what you are doing, where you are, who you are with."

"I disagree," Cal said. "With all due respect of course," she added. "But it is a strong rule of common good claims practice that you never, ever, break off during certain interviews. Taped or not. When they get talking, it takes thirty to sixty minutes to regain lost ground and build back the rapport you have established. In some cases, you might never regain it."

There was a very long minute as the two women regarded each other like gladiators in the coliseum; Cal could almost smell the rotting carcasses of those who had died there before her.

"In those circumstances, I will expect you to call me as soon as it is feasible. Of course, you will report what you were in the middle of."

"Of course," said Cal, knowing she had won the skirmish, but not wanting the war. "I'm impressed that you have so much expertise, Carmen, I look forward to learning from you."

"You don't learn in this business, Calistoga. Either you're an investigator or you're not."

"Cal is short for California," Cal said.

"We will pay you for Friday." Carmen went on, ignoring her. "But there will be no more wild-goose chases."

"Not a one." Cal shook her head, but it refused to follow her brain's directions. Everything was going south.

"Now let's get down to business—your first assignment for Worldwide—you're going to do some traveling."

• • •

Carmen buzzed Linda on the intercom. A second later, Linda burst through the door.

"Yes . . . ma'am." She was trembling.

"Linda, you need not appear in person when I buzz. A simple opening of the connection on your side will suffice." Linda gave her a quizzical look.

"Buzz me back," Carmen said with a steely edge to her voice.

"Yes, ma'am." Linda nearly curtsied.

"And you can call me Ms. DeMille. No ma'ams. Sounds like we're home on the range."

"Yes, ma'am, Ms. DeMille," Linda was close to derailing.

"Tell Denny Norm he can come in now and meet California."

"California?" Linda looked carsick.

"Me," said Cal simply.

Linda fled. Two minutes later a handsome tanned blond man appeared in the doorway. Carmen smiled her first sincere smile of the morning. The gold cross swayed.

"Denny, this is Cal. You both will be working this new assignment together."

"Dennis Norman Wickerstaff, pleased to meet you," he said, extending his hand. Cal shook it, testing its grip, which was neither friendly nor polite. It was a handshake that bespoke absolute control. His eyes glinted like metal on a winter's day.

"Must be a big case," Cal noted aloud, "two investigators."

"You'll be learning our field procedures. A bit different

than the Underhill way." Carmen licked her lips. "Denny's ex-L.A.P.D."

In a dazzling ball of brilliant light, Cal realized what was going down: Denny was the investigator. She was going along for the ride. And Denny would bear witness against her when she broke one of the myriad of rules Worldwide was probably so fond of.

As if reading her mind, Carmen walked over to her desk and picked up an enormous looseleaf binder, which she handed to Cal. "Read it," said Carmen. Her eyes were mad like Rasputin's. "Our manual," she added with almost religious fervor.

"Read it and weep," said Denny. He could say anything. Cal was history.

Beads of sweat had broken out on Carmen's upper lip, as if Denny being in the room raised the temperature. Her gold cross flashed Morse at him.

On the other side of the door Linda dropped something terribly heavy; neither Carmen nor Denny flinched. Cal too, stood her ground; she'd have to, as an even truer test of her mettle was definitely in her future.

6

"RENO, OH, RENO." LAURIE danced around Cal's living room. She balanced a bowl of fruit on her head, holding it with one hand, then swung it down in order to pop a grape into her mouth.

"Careful of the Fiesta ware, it's vintage," Cal warned, "and I don't know why you're so excited. You make it sound like Rio. It's only Nevada."

"Getting out of town, you lucky thing. Tuesday morning, nine A.M. and *I'll* be chained to my drawing board, quill in hand, at Industrial Light and Magic."

"I thought you loved your job."

Laurie sat down heavily on the couch. "But to be on the road. On the road again!" Her blue eyeshadow made her look like a doleful peacock.

"You know, really, buddy, it's not all it's cracked up to be."

"Pine forests and canyons."

"Trapped in blizzards. Tornadoes and thunderstorms."

"Deer and eagles."

"Bears and mountain lions."

"Swiftly running mountain streams."

"Searching for a rest room."

"Freedom! Freedom!"

"Yeah, locked in a car with ex-L.A.P.D."

"Is he cute?"

"As cute as the Donner Pass was to the settlers who tried to cross it a hundred or so years ago."

"Wasn't that where? . . ."

"Yeah, that's the spot. And I'm sure my experience will be somewhat similar. I can imagine all the neuroses this guy has. He'll be carrying more baggage than me!"

"But Reno, Cal. Isn't that the greatest little city in the world? I saw it in a Clint Eastwood movie."

"Life doesn't always imitate art, Laur. Besides, this guy isn't exactly Clint Eastwood. My days are numbered at this company anyway."

"Are you going to quit?" Laurie followed Cal as she went to the hall closet and took out a suitcase with wheels.

"No. I'm not going to give them the satisfaction." Cal struggled with both the suitcase and the subject.

"Can I help you pack?"

"I don't need any disguises on this case, Laur," Cal zipped open the luggage and began placing items inside. "This is an insurance investigation into an accidental death."

"How do you investigate a death? Take the red dress, for the casino."

"I am *not* there to have fun," Cal said firmly, and eyed her friend with irritation.

"Work, work, work," Laurie chided, but she knew Cal disliked having too much spare time on her hands. That gave her too much time to think, Cal had once confided, and when she did, depression rushed in to take hold. Cal also had remarked that she had tried depression and it had depressed her. "Maybe the only way, Cal, is to slow down." Laurie really wanted to help her.

"I don't want to," Cal said.

"But you need to—so you can move on." Laurie took the red dress out of the closet and, hanger and all, placed it in the suitcase. Cal didn't protest. Laurie took this as a sign to proceed. "You need to, Cal, so you can live a normal life again."

Cal smoothed the dress but didn't look up. "I'm not normal now?"

"Look, for example, take Steve."

"Orella? Nah, you take Steve."

"Cal, I would if I could. But honey, wake up. It's you he has the hots for."

"So what?" Cal took her hiking boots out of the closet and placed them next to the suitcase. "Maybe I need another suitcase for the shoes."

"Yeah, take that soft-sided tapestry one," Laurie said. "But you're changing the subject."

"No, I'm playing coy. But only for a little while. Then I'll snare him, hook, line, and sinker. And reel him in like a barracuda. Watch out for the teeth!"

"I can see you learned a lot in Florida."

"And I'll have David declared legally dead, which he probably is by now anyway. And Steve and I will get married. And then, with my luck, something really weird and unforseen will happen to him too."

Laurie looked at her friend sadly. People could never see clearly into their own actions. Or sometimes they did but were powerless to act on them. "Why won't you be happy?"

"Because I'm not meant to be happy. But I am happy."

"That has an odd, convoluted sense of truth to it, but I can't figure out where it's flawed. You can't be happy but you're happy!" Laurie threw her hands up. "Give it a chance, girl."

"And then I open up, open myself up. To being left. Again."

"But nobody knows what happened to David," Laurie said.

"I couldn't stand to go through that again." Cal kept throwing outfits into the suitcase to avoid Laurie's eyes.

"It *was* pretty sudden. He just went out for cigarettes—"

"And never came back. I don't know if I'll ever stop asking myself, was it something I did?"

"Take that sweater," Laurie said quickly, on the verge of tears.

"I don't want to look for Mr. Right anymore. Mr. Right *Now* would be better."

"Cal!" Laurie exclaimed.

"I've changed in a hundred ways. I know that I'm not the same person I was seven years ago."

"None of us are, Cal."

"What I mean is, I'm not strong. David's disappearing act took something vital out of me. Some core of inner strength I used to have."

"Cal, stop. You're the hardest on yourself. You're the strongest woman I know."

"No, I'm—Laurie, the sauce!"

They both rushed into the kitchen.

"It's okay," Cal said as she lowered the heat and stirred, "we caught it in time. David hated my cooking. We almost always ate out."

"But you're an incredible cook."

"I've learned how to cook. A natural progression. Almost . . . as if . . . he comes back someday, I could cook for him." Laurie nodded. "I remember the first time I made a meatloaf. I packed it into this toaster oven, and left it. The gravy was all over the countertop, the floor!" Cal's eyes focused on a distant spot on the wall. "Those were my days of inno-cence."

"Innocent meatloaf?" Laurie said.

"Laurie, only you can get me to laugh," Cal said.

"It's a start. Tell me about the new case."

"I'll tell you what I can without violating confidentiality— a little kid died. He got stuck somehow in an escalator in one of the casinos."

"No! Don't tell me anymore. I'm sorry I asked. I don't know how you stand all this blood-and-guts stuff. Maybe I should be happy I'm chained to a drawing board." Laurie walked back into the living room. Cal gave the spaghetti sauce one final stir and followed her.

"Oh! A video. Are we watching a movie tonight?" Laurie held up the package Cal's secretary Linda had given her two days ago. Cal had ripped off the top portion of the wrapping. "Do we have any time to watch before dinner? Chuck Norris. A self-defense workout tape. Neat!"

"My secretary arms me like Q looks after James Bond. Go ahead," Cal said. "Put it on." Cal wandered back into the kitchen and went to work on the pasta.

"I want to push the button on the pasta machine," Laurie called from the living room. " 'Attitude, awareness, and being prepared,' " she repeated after Chuck Norris. " 'Enhance awareness and inner strength.' Cal, c'mere. He talks about inner strength. This is no ordinary video."

"Aerobics make you lean," said Chuck Norris, from the screen. "I'm going to make you lean and mean."

"Cal, get in here," Laurie yelled.

Cal came back in. "I've got to put the pasta dough up."

"Forget the pasta, you've got to see this!"

"It must be good to get you to say forget the pasta." Cal sat down. Laurie immediately jumped up as Norris began to demonstrate various defensive postures.

"Cal, c'mon. Oh, wait. I forgot your neck and back."

Cal didn't even want to shake her head. "My mind says yes, but my body definitely says no."

"Step forward, left foot," Laurie repeated. "How to punch properly. Cal, watch!"

"I'm watching, I'm watching."

" 'Aim for his nose,' " Laurie said. " 'Your breaking hand is the left. Shattering hand the right.' " Laurie began to punch the air. " 'Turn the hips, this is where the power comes from, even if you are the weaker of the two,' " she repeated. " 'Break, and then shatter.' I'm feeling meaner every second."

"Very impressive," Cal said, wincing as she shifted position on the couch. "As I learn the true meaning of the expression 'couch pasta.' "

"Break and shatter," Laurie kept saying.

"Remember," said Norris from the screen, "the whole purpose is to get away from this confrontation."

"Mean and lean. Mean. Mean," said Laurie. "Oh, now the kicks."

The phone rang.

Cal got up, watching the screen and looking at Laurie as she snatched up the receiver. She spoke for about fifteen minutes, her voice low and somber. Then she started to write on a pad she kept by the phone. When she hung up she returned to her position on the couch, her face an expressionless mask.

"Hey, couch pasta. Is everything okay?" Laurie was doing kicks now.

"No. Everything is far from okay."

"What's up?" Laurie abandoned her karate stance.

"It's Tony. Tony Lazio. You remember him?"

"That guy with the gorgeous eyes you used to date in high school? The one that broke into your apartment while you were asleep a few months ago?"

"One and the same," said Cal.

"Was that him on the phone?" asked Laurie.

"That was his mom. She was calling from the hospital."

"Tony's—"

"No. Tony's not in the hospital. His dad's had another heart attack. She didn't know who to call. She couldn't tell Frank the latest—" Cal covered her eyes and shook her head.

Laurie sat down next to her. "What? What happened?"

"Tony's going to kill himself. She got a letter from him in the mail today. It's pretty much a suicide note."

"Do you think he means it, Cal?"

"He threatens in a very Tony kind of way. Sometimes Tony can be very, well, emotional. But from what I've read about people threatening suicide, you're supposed to take them very seriously."

"So what you're saying is, that even though Tony can exaggerate at times, he might very well mean it."

"This is a major cry for help. I saw Tony at the anniversary party this past Saturday. He's fallen off the wagon big-time. He was acting looped. I couldn't tell if he was drinking or if he was on something. He acted wild. Wild words, wild actions."

"And now this," said Laurie. "Can you do anything?"

"That's why Mrs. Lazio called. These people are like family to me. Tony was my first love. When people start having problems, that's when they really need you."

"But, Cal. Tony hasn't just started to have problems. From what you've told me, he's been on a slide downhill for quite a while. He killed that girl when he was driving drunk."

"Listen to his note—his mother read it to me and I wrote it down:

" 'Dear Mom and Dad,
Mom, I ask that somehow you break this news to Dad. Please choose the right time, I don't want him getting sick over me.

Since I got out of jail, I've found I can't get back into life on the outside. I've been so down, I know I can't ever get back up.

I'm leaving California. I don't want to be there for the short time I have left. I want to go out in style, my own time, my choosing.

I'm sorry if I've caused you any pain, but my pain is more than I can handle.

Give my collection of comics to Cal. Tell her I've never stopped loving her.

This is good-bye.

Your son,

Tony.' "

"Wow," said Laurie. "That's heavy duty."

"Mrs. Lazio says she thinks he'd head for Nevada. He loves to gamble. I said I would try and help, that I was leaving for Nevada myself in the morning on a case."

"What about the police?"

"She's called them. He's not on parole and since he left

the state it's out of their jurisdiction. She also tried Nevada. They said they didn't have the manpower to look for every guy who wrote a sad note to his mother."

"Damn bureaucracy."

"Mrs. Lazio called the hospitals and jails. I told her to get me his credit card numbers. Luckily she's got a key to his place. She's going to see if she can find any old receipts or statements."

"I can just imagine Tony's filing system," said Laurie.

"Really."

"Then?" asked Laurie.

"Then I'll track him down. Get him some help."

"What about giving you his comics?"

"That was almost the scariest part of the letter. Tony has these comics from the forties and fifties. His collection is awesome. I'll find him. I will," she added.

Hopefully, Laurie thought, *before it's too late.*

7

CAL DIDN'T LIKE VERY early mornings. It was dark, she felt as if she had been up all night, instead of waking in the first moments of a brand-new day.

Dawn crept up on them hesitantly, all grayness and patchy fog as they headed north on 101. Cal was driving; they had decided to take her Firebird.

"Want to stop for coffee and doughnuts?" she asked as they neared San Rafael.

Denny slouched in the passenger seat, dark gray hollows under his eyes matching the light. But even in the gloom of the car interior his hair gleamed, an impeccable blond helmet, every hair feathered and anchored in place.

"I don't like cop jokes." He spoke without moving his lips. Not a good sign. "And where's all the traffic?"

"I never thought I'd hear someone complain about lack of traffic. But that's how I planned it." Cal tried to be cheerful. "We'll loop around on 37. You think this road's empty, wait'll you see that one."

"There's no one up here, 'cause there's nothing up here," Denny said, looking disdainfully at the passing scenery that was just beginning to be revealed in the growing light. "I never should have left L.A.," he said. "Only cops can make cop jokes," he added sourly.

Cal kept her eyes on the road; she didn't want to risk looking at him with his bottomless-pit been-to-hell-and-back gaze. "That wasn't a joke. I thought we could stop and get something. I went to Marine World once with my dad and we stopped up around here and got some doughnuts."

"I remind you of your dad?"

Cal could see where this was going; he was uncomfortable around her but had roused himself to the effort of projecting it back upon her. "You sound like a cup of coffee wouldn't hurt." She made one last attempt to make the peace.

"Don't want to stop. You're driving like an old lady. Step on it!"

It was then that Cal realized she had been locked in a car going north up 101 with the devil. "I don't want to get a ticket," she protested.

His laugh was driven by demons. Cal wondered what they were; then she didn't want to find out.

His gray gaze ran over her hotly, then coldly. Hot and cold, that was his game.

"Pull over. I'll drive."

"In a while," she countered. "Maybe we'll stop in a place with a restroom. Okay?" Cal liked to drive first leg of a trip, while she was fresh.

"Women. Fuck. Can't take 'em anywhere. They need to take a crap every ten miles."

Cal thought daggers at him. Her back had started to feel as if it were twisted up like a question mark. She couldn't say anything about that.

He'd never get to know the real Cal Brantley. Not that she wanted him to. She had her hidden agendas, thinking of the picture she had placed in her wallet last night. Tony, age thirteen. His eyes were the brilliant color of his turquoise shirt and he was wearing the ID bracelet he'd give to her the following spring. The large linked bracelet that she had unearthed from her old jewelry box and wore this morning.

Up ahead was a sign that simply announced Eats.

"Here we go," she said cheerfully, gritting her teeth.

Tony's mother was at the first phone number she had given Cal the night before. A statement from the credit card company had been in Tony's mail; she read off the number to Cal.

"Gigi, Gigi, be there." Cal crossed her fingers as she made her next phone call. She was on her cell phone in a stall in the ladies' room, the only place she was sure Denny wouldn't follow.

"Gigi!" she exclaimed as her cousin came on the line. "I need your help. I need you to find Tony Lazio before he goes and does something stupid." Cal went on briefly to outline what had happened, and swore her cousin to secrecy. Her family was prone to gossip, and the Lazios had enough problems for the time being.

"Cal, we do find people. But usually I turn it over to the bounty hunter."

"I thought you'd be able to track them down with credit card information."

"To tell you the truth—I don't know what the bounty hunter does. But our clients sign something when they, or the cosigner, post the bond. Gives us permission to get into their credit."

Cal thought quickly; Tony hadn't signed anything and here she was, asking Gigi to get into his credit records.

"Actually, the bounty hunter doesn't like to be called that any more. He calls himself a recovery specialist. Skip tracer."

"Gigi, listen. Thanks. Sorry I bothered you. I'll get it done some other way."

She dialed again. "C'mon. Answer the phone."

A strange voice came on the line; so much for just replacing management. "Orella!" Cal bit out the word.

"I'll connect," came a just-as-terse reply.

"Steve!" she said as soon as she heard his voice.

"Cal! You sound almost glad to talk to me," he said. "How's the neck?"

"I can't talk," she whispered in nearly a croak. She cleared her throat and said again, "I can't talk. I'm on my way to Reno with this investigator Worldwide sent up from L.A."

"I heard about that."

Cal knew from the way Orella said "heard" that he wanted to talk. She wished she could. "I need a favor," she said anxiously.

"Favors are in short supply these days. They're watching

our every move," he said in a very low voice. "All the Underhill people."

"This guy they sent up—"

"What's his name?" asked Orella.

"Denny Norman Wickerstaff."

"Wonder where they got him from," said Orella.

"Ex-L.A.P.D."

"Lucky you."

"Listen, I got to go. He's timing me, I swear. I need you to run this credit card number for me. I need a printout of all current charges." Cal read off the number.

"The feds are coming down hard on exactly this kind of stuff, Cal."

"Remember that guy at the party? Tony. Tony Lazio?"

"Now, who could forget that loser? Oh, excuse me, wasn't he your old boyfriend? Why didn't you give the guy a second chance?"

"Restaurants get two chances. Men only get one. He's in trouble with a capital *T*."

"Why do I feel so happy?"

"He's threatened suicide, Steve. This is—oh, darn. There's a weird noise. I swear—"

The door to the ladies room thudded open and from the bottom of her stall, Cal could see the pointed toes of Denny's black boots. She disconnected the connection to Orella and flushed the toilet.

"Cal!" Denny said in a loud voice. "If we don't get this show on the road, there's going to be hell to pay!"

Cal swung open the stall door. Denny stood there, thumbs

hooked in the belt loops of his jeans, a Heineken cradled in his other four fingers of one hand. Poster boy for the American justice system.

"What are you going to do," Cal said, "shoot me?"

"Maybe," came the response.

He drove as if they were in a pursuit. It was the pure cops' version of traveling. Ninety miles an hour, weaving in and out of traffic. All they lacked was the siren.

"This is driving," he said, after they had covered about thirty-five miles. Cal didn't say anything. "What's the worst could happen?" he said, looking at her for a too-long minute. "We get pulled over. I flash 'em this." Denny dug his wallet out of a back pocket, pulled out a card with his teeth, and tossed it in her lap. It was his proof: retired cop, L.A.P.D. Concealed weapon permit. He flashed her a rare grin.

"You get a pension?" she asked, hoping to see a winsome smile again.

"Fuck, yeah. Also, my lawsuit money's comin' in. Against the main man, Gates, Mr. Chief-of-Police himself. Eight hundred thou. They took me off the promotion list."

Cal didn't say a word.

The scenery went by like a movie in fast forward. Soon, a sign read Sacramento 11 Miles.

"We'll take the turnoff for Highway 80," Cal said, her California *Thomas Guide* in her lap.

"You're the navigator," Denny said in a nearly normal tone. "Just don't get us fucking lost."

At least this wasn't a date. It was an idea she needed to firmly hang on to.

"You've got a gun on you right now?"

"Does Dolly Parton sleep on her back? I got three." He was in his element now.

"Mind if I ask where? How?"

"Shoulder holster. Throwaway piece on my right calf. And a neat little number that sort of tumbles down my sleeve."

"Then we should be very safe," Cal said, wondering who would protect her against *him*.

"Safe. You don't need a weapon to be safe. I got my own bare hands. These are killing hands." Denny held them up, off the wheel. Cal made a mighty effort and repressed a shudder at the double scenario: the car swerving off the road and/ or Denny killing with his bare hands. She couldn't decide which was nastier.

"We're in this bar, see. Me and my woman. And this guy elbows her. She takes me aside and tells me he did it on purpose. I go confront the dude. He gets hostile. I put him in a choke hold. Squeeze just a bit too much in the right place. Damn, I had that hold down pat, perfect form. Next thing I know . . ." Denny didn't finish the sentence.

Cal looked over at him, swallowed hard.

He looked at her, grinned.

Shivers, exploding up and down Cal's spine.

"Yup, dead. I killed him." Denny's face was a study in contrasts. The grin, those eyes. Cal felt she had just stepped off the midway at a carnival and entered the freak show area. Her breath caught in her throat; she couldn't breathe in, she couldn't exhale.

"Fucker fucked with me, he's fucked," said Denny.

8

CAL REACHED FOR THE radio dial, clicked it on. She fiddled with the dial till she got a hard-rock oldies station. Led Zeppelin came on.

"Be warned, lady, I don't go in for none of this sexual harassment shit. You fuck with me, your ass is cooked. You run with wolves you're one of the pack. Sacramento, shit. Where are the fucking buildings?"

"Okay," said Cal, relieved that her breathing was proceeding of its own volition. "Here comes the turnoff. Bear right, yeah, bear all the way."

"One hick town. Get me the fuck out of here, wheels." Denny pressed on the gas, the speedometer cresting the hundred mark, one ten, and he left the state capital in his dust.

"Faster we get there," Denny said, "faster I can show you how a real investigation's done."

Cal tuned him out, listening to Robert Plant singing, John Bonham on drums. Denny reached over, just as Plant was really getting whipped up, and flicked the radio off.

"That music was what done this nation in," Denny said.

It was then, that very moment, that Cal knew she really hated him.

He fell silent after that and the road grew more curved; he was taking the turns as though he was playing with a Matchbox car. There were pine trees now and the air grew clearer but colder.

"I seen things would make you puke," Denny picked up the thread of his hour-long monologue. "Donner Pass," he read off the next road sign. "Ain't there a place around here a man can get some refreshment?"

There was no way Cal was going to let him in on the joke.

"I hate all this damn nature," Denny said, several minutes later. "Trees, rocks, trees. Get me back to civilization."

Amen, thought Cal.

They got into Reno shortly after, stopping first at a sprawling complex called Boomtown. Denny's lunch was mostly liquid accompanied by a steak sandwich. Cal picked at a salad.

"Are you one of them bulimics?" Denny prodded.

"I'm a vegetarian," Cal said.

"One of those animal rights advocates?" asked Denny.

Cal wondered if everything she said was being transmitted to Worldwide headquarters. Even if he wasn't recording her, he would tell them whatever it was they needed to know.

Her neck throbbed steadily now, after the toboggan trip.

"Well, I like my steak," he said, neatly pushing the last of his sandwich into his mouth and signaling the waitress for another beer.

Cal's bag was partly open on the chair next to her and a bottle of Advil was visible; it was her one concession to the auto accident injuries.

"Time of the month." Denny smirked, getting up and snatching the check off the tabletop. He cavalierly handed it to Cal, adding "That explains a lot."

He didn't miss a trick, Cal noted. She'd have to remember that.

They checked into a place called the Lucky Motel, in the running for the dive-of-the-month award. If one of the road clubs ever stopped in to rate it, they'd run out in hysterics.

"We'll have more money for food and such with the per diem expense account," Denny said.

A sign in the office window advertised hourly rates. Cal didn't unpack.

9

CAL OPENED THE GLASS door to the casino. Denny was right behind her, swaggering in with his cowboy boots and jeans. As they made their way past the hordes of gamblers, Cal turned and asked him if they had to be specially licensed to conduct an investigation in Nevada.

"Worldwide is licensed in this state," Denny replied. "Nevada is real strict about California PIs coming in and working here unlicensed." Denny's tone was so cold Cal was sorry she asked a question. She had the feeling she was walking on eggshells, treading very carefully.

Denny was a trip, no doubt about it, but he hadn't crossed her personal line. And, she reminded herself, in a way Worldwide was picking up the tab as she attempted to contact Tony. She smiled at the thought of breaking loose, in some way, from Denny's tight control.

"Where do I find the head honcho?" he demanded now of an employee walking by.

"Is there a problem?"

Denny acted as though his method of ex-cop bravado worked on everyone. What he didn't realize, thought Cal, was that insurance work was different from police work. Many times she had conducted witness canvasses in cases where the police, there before her, had turned up little. But it seemed that the people she talked to, even children, couldn't wait to tell her what was really happening or what had gone down.

"I need to see the people who run this show," said Denny, glaring at the woman, who had actually retreated several inches.

"We need to speak with Mr. Tsakopoulos." Cal broke in with a smile. "Is that how you pronounce it?"

The employee's discomfort level visibly dropped. "Sure, go right, up that hallway, left, then another left after you go through the large double doors."

Denny was off, Cal at his heels. "Right, left, goddamn obstacle course," he was muttering. He nearly ran into an elderly man breathing through an oxygen canister strapped on his back.

"Spending the inheritance." Denny commented, turning to Cal. She looked quickly away from the barely alive wreck of a person and Denny's flushed angry face. *That's what Denny's soul looks like* she thought.

"We had an appointment." Denny actually pounded the receptionist's desk when they were told that the person they asked to see was out.

The receptionist was clearly flustered as she checked her computer screen for guidance. Cal knew they didn't have an exact time but had informed management they would be in sometime on Tuesday. Denny looked as if he was going to whip out his old police ID card and attempt to intimidate the woman even more.

"We're here regarding that accident on the escalator last month. The little boy," Cal said in a low, friendly voice.

"The little boy," said the receptionist sadly, turning to speak with Cal. "Are you—" She started to say something, but then thought the better of it, putting the back of one hand to her mouth.

"I'm Cal Brantley, and this is Denny Wickerstaff of Worldwide Investigations. We're here on behalf of your insurance company."

"Oh," was all the receptionist could say, relieved.

Cal handed her a business card. "That's my old card. We're having new ones printed up."

"I'll see who can help you. Sorry about the problem with the appointment," the woman said, speaking to Cal. "Have a seat, please."

Cal sat, showing Denny how it was done. Denny paced.

"Sit down," Cal said to Denny pleasantly. She felt like she was giving commands to a pitbull.

After a short wait, a slender man with very white skin and Buddy Holly glasses came out of one of the inner offices. Cal knew Denny was immediately sizing him up; she was getting to know his moves. With women and the elderly and short men he was an aggressor, an animal. Cal waited to see what happened when he came up against someone who wasn't in one of those categories. In fact, she positively looked forward to the experience; it promised to be quite interesting, or at the very least, instructive.

"Mr. Brantley, I'm—" the man said, offering his hand, which Denny pointedly ignored.

"No, I'm Miss Brantley. Cal Brantley," Cal said, standing up.

"I'm Rick Bronson," he said, a flush immediately suffusing his cheeks. Denny was shaking his head as if Bronson was beyond redemption. Cal had the overwhelming urge to laugh; she felt it was either that or have a heart attack. "And you're both—" Bronson couldn't finish the sentence, Denny was making him so nervous. Cal knew the feeling as she stifled a chuckle.

"We're both investigators," she told him. "We're here on behalf of your insurance carrier—the escalator case. The child who . . ." Cal said.

"Yes, yes. We're aware of why you're here." Bronson threw a worried look in the direction of the receptionist as if at any minute she'd say she'd had enough and leave. Cal knew that feeling too. "I'm the head accountant."

Denny gave him the appropriate incredulous look. Bronson tried to ignore him. "I've been instructed to fully cooperate with you until Mr. T. arrives. Have you checked into your rooms?"

"Yes," said Cal. Denny wasn't going to say a word.

"Were they to your liking?"

"Well . . ." Cal paused.

"Is there anything we can do? Move you to a different floor, perhaps—"

"Oh, we're not staying here," Cal said as casually as she could.

"You're not?"

"You say you're an accountant. Ever hear of a budget?" Denny was getting warmed up.

"Here comes Mr. T. now," said Bronson, his voice cracking with relief.

"I'm Alex Tsakopoulos," said the distinguished-looking man, offering a hand that glistened with a sizable gold ring and a heavy gold Rolex. He appeared to be in his early thirties with prematurely gray hair. He had a neatly trimmed salt-and-pepper beard and mustache.

Cal shook the proffered hand. Mr. T. had strikingly blue eyes, which met hers for a moment, then drifted leisurely down, then back up again, taking her all in. Cal felt complimented, but she shot a worried glance over at Denny, who was scowling in the corner. She introduced herself and then Denny.

Mr. T. led them out of the reception area into his own office. "Where do you want to begin?" he said in a smooth voice.

"We have the report you filed," Cal said. "We're basically here to look into what happened and to interview witnesses face-to-face. Is there anything else that you can think of that wasn't covered in the report?"

Alex scanned a duplicate of the document Cal had in her file. "I know this is most likely unconnected to the accident, but we had a robbery and subsequent murder that same day."

"Murder!" Cal's eyebrows rose quizzically up.

"One of the cocktail waitresses, Dawn, was found slain outside in the alley near a service entrance. Police said it was robbery related. Her cash tips were not found on her person and it was nearing the end of her shift."

"What a terrible, tragic day," Cal said. She made a swift entry on a pad of paper. "Dawn—what was her last name?"

"Delaney. Dawn Delaney."

"And the police said they saw no connection to the child's accident on the escalator?"

"None whatsoever."

"I think, first, we should see the escalator where the fatality occurred."

"Cal!" Denny barked out her name suddenly. When Cal looked over, he motioned her to a corner of the room.

"What's up?" she asked.

"I say we cut to the chase. Interview the pit boss, see the kid's mother, and wind this up."

"You won't have anything in your report." Cal tried to be tactful.

"It's all bullshit," said Denny. "Dead is dead."

"We better interview some additional witnesses," Cal said, disagreeing but trying to appear as if she wasn't.

"Who cares what anyone saw?" said Denny. "What they need is an escalator expert."

"Good idea," said Cal. "But let's do some witnesses for the hell of it."

"Okay. Drag it out then."

Cal returned to the waiting man.

"After you, Mr. T.," she said.

He smiled at her. "Call me Alex," he said.

They rode down the escalator, Cal in the lead.

"How long have you worked for the casino, Mr. Tsak-opoulos?" Denny asked.

"I own the casino, Mr.—"

"You can call me Denny."

"You can call me Mr. Tsakopoulos."

They had all reached the bottom of the escalator and Denny and Alex regarded each other like two cobras that had just arisen out of separate baskets.

"The escalator we just rode down on is the one, Miss Brantley," said Alex.

"Cal, please," she said, repressing a shiver.

"As you can see, nothing is wrong with the escalator. We notified the manufacturer immediately after the accident and two representatives and their most experienced techs came out. I have a copy of their report."

"Mr. Tsakopoulos." Denny stood there with his arms folded across his chest. "Let's take it from the top. Now, as I understand it, the kid is DOA at the hospital. What, if anything, did the casino do to try and save him?"

Tsakopoulos was immediately on the defensive. "Well, we called emergency immediately—"

"Did anyone give the kid CPR?"

"No, I don't think—"

"Do you have anyone certified on staff for emergencies?"

"No—"

"Do you have a health and safety officer?"

"No—"

"A nurse?"

"No."

"A doctor?"

"For purposes of liability, we don't—"

"Seems like we got some liability on us now," said Denny, a mean glint coming into his eye at Alex's discomfort.

"Denny," Cal broke in, "it's not for us to apportion liability."

"Just going over the basics with Mr. Tsakopoulos. Now, I'll need the names of all employees who were witnesses." Denny was issuing orders like a drill sergeant.

"There's the pit boss, Justin LaSchiaffa."

"Okay, we got this Justin. He here today?"

"Justin's out on stress leave. He is represented by an attorney."

"Then we can't talk with him," Denny said with finality.

"No," said Cal, "if he's rep for the comp case we can speak with him regarding the actual incident and what he witnessed. We can call his lawyer and get permission. In fact, to be on the safe side, we'll make certain his lawyer is present."

Alex looked at her as if she were brilliant; admiringly, whether for her efficiency or her body was not clear. Denny glared. "Okay, okay, who else?" Denny said.

"Actually, it all happened pretty fast. No one else has come forward."

"Well, that's gonna look real good. A kid dies on the floor of your casino and no one except one person sees anything."

Alex shook his head, looking more worried by the minute.

"Let's start with a schedule of employees who were on duty during that shift," Cal said. "Then we can see what their proximity was to the escalator."

"There was also an eyewitness who was a casino patron," Alex said.

"How was he involved?" Denny asked.

"According to the written report supplied by Justin, the patron tried to free up the youngster with his knife," said Alex in a low voice as if he already knew what Denny's response was going to be.

Denny didn't disappoint. "Mama mia," he exclaimed, clapping a hand to his forehead.

"We'll need a copy of that report," said Cal, trying to keep them on track. "Hopefully, someone has this person's phone number and address."

"Hopefully," said Denny.

"When do you think it's a good time to take some pictures?" Cal asked.

"I saw a sign that said No Strollers and Hold All Children by the Hand," Denny interrupted as if he had discovered gold.

"You think you'll find something that will help our side, Cal?" asked Alex.

"I'd like to try and answer your question," Cal replied. "I think it's important from the start of this investigation that I tell you even though you're our client, I'm going to be neutral. *We* will be neutral." Cal was really trying. "This way if something comes up, we can see it more clearly. No preconceived notions getting in the way. Also, we're not attorneys. We don't know how the evidence can be introduced, or even if it's relevant. So, we simply try to do a thorough investigation and just gather the facts as they are presented to us."

"That sounds fair," Alex replied. "Oh, about the pictures. You asked when it was a good time. Fact is, the casino is never empty. Always a crowd, even at four in the morning. So take your pictures any time you want. No one will notice."

"They didn't seem to notice when the kid died either," said Denny.

Both Alex and Cal ignored him.

"Let's go back upstairs," said Cal, "and pick up those additional reports and witness names. Denny and I will also get the police report as well as Fire and Rescue. For the ambulance we'll have to get a release from the parents. Do you know if they're represented?"

"As far as we know, there's only a mother. No father's name has come up. And no, the mother hasn't said anything about lawyers getting involved. Is that good?"

"Controlled claimants can sometimes be the most difficult," replied Cal.

"All they want is the green poultice," said Denny. "Insurance lingo," he added.

"Mr. Wickerstaff's background is L.A.P.D.," Cal said.

"That explains a lot," said Alex under his breath.

" 'Scuse me," Denny wasn't going to let it go.

"Just a joke," said Alex defensively.

"This here's no joke, Tsakopoulos. Seems to me you and your people should have taken what went on here a lot more seriously. Maybe the kid would still be alive. And you, what're you staring at?"

Cal was looking at the spot where the boy's jacket had become stuck. "A place where someone died. It makes me feel—weird. You know." She looked at Alex, who met her eyes.

"I think I know how you feel," he replied. "Sometimes I feel that way about this whole town."

10

"RIDICULOUS," DENNY EXCLAIMED WHEN Cal said she needed to take pictures riding back down the escalator. She had already shot an entire roll of the accident site, including close-ups of the escalator steps and a panoramic view, by quadrants.

Cal ignored him and went ahead. It only took a few minutes but when they retreated to the small office provided by the casino, Denny was seething. His eyes were slightly bloodshot as he tilted backward in his chair and looked over at her with disdain. He had his arms linked in back of his head and his biceps bulged solidly. Cal kept her eyes on his face.

"You'll build this bill up to several thousand," he said.

"I'm not building anything. I'm just doing a basic investigation," Cal answered calmly.

"Well, Sherlock. Since you're so experienced, what next?"

"The casino's security cameras are probably just trained

on the gaming tables. That's probably a dead end. So let's contact the local cops," Cal said, as if she were offering a small child an ice cream. It worked. Denny's face lost some of its tension and he reached for the phone with a sparkle coming back into his eyes. Cal took out the file and began to document notes on the investigation to date.

He had just finished a loud and lengthy conversation sprinkled with profanities, when Cal's beeper went off.

"Why they callin' you?" Denny demanded. "Worldwide should be pagin' me. I'm in charge."

Cal reluctantly checked the number on the pager screen.

"It's someone from L.A. I called them before to check on some computer stuff for me." She was trying hard to appear casual.

"Old case?" Denny's antenna was up. Careful, thought Cal; he was snooping.

"Yeah, some loose ends."

Denny looked at her. She sat there, not making a move toward the phone.

"Well," he said, "make the call."

"I don't want to call from here. Why should they pay for it? It's not their case."

Denny smirked.

"I'll be back in a minute," she said, forcing herself to stand up and walk out the door. She found a pay phone.

"Orella, you got anything for me?"

"Cal, this must be your lucky day. He's using his card. As of yesterday, Lazio is at the Four Aces Motel. Right in Reno."

Cal breathed a sigh of relief as her entire body went limp. "Now all I have to do is shake Denny and make contact with Tony."

"Do you have a game plan after that?"

"No, I haven't really thought it out. But I'm hoping Tony'll listen to me."

"He seems like one angry dude."

"He's angry at himself."

"Just be careful."

"He'd never hurt me. It's himself he wants to harm."

"Just remember, Cal, lie down with dogs, you get nothing but fleas."

"Thanks for the advice, Orella. But what's it got to do with Tony? Maybe you've been spending too much time with Mighty Dog."

"Cal, look—"

"You look, Orella. The only real problem here is this Denny guy. He's got a sewer mouth and watches me like a hawk. Gives me the double creeps." Cal looked around nervously as she spoke.

"He put the moves on you?" Orella said, with a real note of concern.

"Nah. Not at all. He doesn't seem to be that way. More like he's watching me so he can have some proof I'm messing up."

"Take care of yourself. Call me if you need anything more."

"Thanks, Steve," Cal said, and hung up, hoping she'd be able to keep both herself and Orella from having to get into the credit card records again. What would Denny do with *that* bit of information?

She walked back down the hallway and smiled at the receptionist, who in turn only looked uncomfortable. Denny was standing in the doorway.

"Finished with your personal call yet?"

"I told you, it was about another case." Her mind was racing. "A ten-minute break."

"Grab your Easter bonnet," he said, a self-satisfied look tempering the coldness of his entire countenance, "we're going to the police station."

"I hope I'm not under arrest," Cal said.

"It could be arranged," he replied.

Denny guided her by the elbow as if he were escorting her to the prom as they went into the police station. He said a few words to the desk sergeant and they were directed through another door, which clinked behind them with an unpleasant sound.

A detective with an enormous stomach greeted Denny, took him aside, and handed him several photocopied papers. They began to confer in low tones and at one point they both broke into loud laughter. Cal could see the cop looking at her out of the corner of his eye. Cop looks.

"There's pictures," Denny finally said to her as if she needed a translator. "Only the family involved can sign a release for most of this stuff since it involves a minor. But Rich here's going to let us take a look-see."

Cal didn't say a word. Rich kept giving her more weasel-eyed looks and she wondered what Denny had told him.

"Also, there's a follow-up report with the names and addresses of the witnesses that hasn't been made available yet. But I told Rich we're only in town for the two days. He's going to make sure we have those too." Rich and Denny exchanged knowing looks as Cal stifled a yawn. If they wanted to feel special, let them. She wasn't going to run out and become a cop, nor did she have plans for a sex change. Both would be required to be in their club.

"Wasn't there a murder the same day at the casino?" Cal asked.

"Yup. Sure kept us busy. Filled out so many forms I had writer's cramp." Rich looked properly peeved.

"Have you solved that one yet?" said Cal.

"Just another ex-whore biting the dust." Rich shrugged.

"She was a former prostitute?" Cal's eyebrows rose a notch.

"Nevada's full of 'em," he replied curtly.

"Is there anything else on the escalator accident?" Cal asked.

Rich wouldn't talk to her directly; again he conferred with Denny.

"They've got the clothes the kid was wearing taken into evidence from the Washoe County coroner's office. But there's like no way we can see that stuff," Denny said. Rich was shaking his head no.

"Look." Cal felt like jerking his chain. "I'm not going back to San Francisco without seeing everything." She

101

wanted to put the pressure on Denny. She wanted to see him fail at something. Anything.

"But Cal, be reasonable—why do we need to see the clothes? What good will that do?"

Cal smiled at both of them innocently. Rich and Denny conferred again, Denny became visibly more agitated as he moved his hands around more, his eyes glazing with frustration. They both looked back over at her.

"Off the record," she said sweetly, "totally off the record."

Rich finally left the room, leaving both Cal and Denny with their gazes locked, trying to stare each other down. Cal was good at this game; she and Gigi used to play it for hours on end throughout their childhood.

Denny blinked first.

Rich came back with a slip of paper, which Denny quickly thrust into his pocket. Rich was also carrying a plastic bag. "Look, but don't touch," he said as he laid it down on the desktop. One by one, he lifted out the items inside.

First there was a pair of boy's sneakers. They were ratty looking and Cal wouldn't have wanted to touch them if she could. Socks. Kid's underwear. Pants. T-shirt. And then the jacket. Rich held it up as if he were doing a magic trick. The string at the neck looked as though it had been gnawed on by animals.

"No blood," remarked Denny. "I seen worse."

Cal looked with interest at the "death" jacket, as she had begun to think of it.

"It looks kind of small for a four-year-old. Why is it so dirty?" she asked of no one in particular.

"Kid was lying on the floor," Rich offered. "Greased up by the escalator machinery."

"Maybe someone stepped on it," said Denny.

"You guys cut the tags out of clothes?" Cal asked, pointing to the raggedly torn label.

"No, we don't touch this stuff," Rich answered.

"Maybe the coroner did?" Cal mused.

"Can't see why," said Rich, who had begun to put the items back into the plastic bag. "Oh, I can't get the pictures till Thursday Denny."

"Shit, that's gonna really hold us up, Rich," Denny said impatiently. "And you"—he turned to Cal—"you ask too many questions."

Cal's pager went off; this time she checked it with a clearer conscience. It was a local call. "We're conducting an investigation," she reminded him.

"The cops investigate. This here's only an insurance claim. It's not a question of whodunit. It's a question of how much—how much cash the insurance carrier's gonna have to pay out." Denny thanked Rich, shook his hand, and turned toward Cal, who was already headed toward the door. Denny, however, looked as though he wanted to stay for roll call.

"Don't you think that was strange, that tag being cut out?" Cal asked as they walked to the car. "Why would someone cut out a tag?"

"You read too many mysteries," Denny said. "Don't mean shit."

"Don't start the car yet," said Cal, "I want to plug in the jack for my car phone."

"Jack shit," replied Denny eyeing his watch. It was clearly getting past the cocktail hour.

Cal dialed the number that had appeared on the pager. "It's Mr. T.," she said, covering the mouthpiece, "he's inviting us to dinner."

"Ha," said Denny, coming back to life, "what's he need me for? It's your pants he wants to get into."

"What should I tell him?" Cal whispered.

"Tell him the hell yes. I never pass up a free meal," Denny said, and started the car.

They rode in silence for a while and when Denny asked her what time dinner was Cal did not immediately answer. She'd been thinking about how to shake Denny loose, get hold of a local directory, and find the Four Aces Motel.

11

"ALEX, DINNER WAS VERY, very good." Cal pushed her
chair back from the table. "Thank you so much." Cal was
self-assured and stunning in the red dress.

"I'll make sure Cal gets back to her room in one piece,"
Denny said quickly. He had drunk enough to kill most men.
It only lowered his voice to a rumbling bass.

"No, don't leave yet," said the casino owner. "I can't
recall when I have had such interesting guests." Here he
paused; possibly the plural of "guest" giving him a bit of
trouble. Nothing got by Denny, the corner of his mouth
turned down a millimeter. Cal wondered what it would take
to render him oblivious.

"Join me, please, for the show. The Righteous Brothers
are our headliners tonight."

"Alex it's been a long day. And tomorrow, we must get
up early—the investigation." Cal reminded him of the reason they were in Reno.

"Show sounds pretty righteous to me, bro," said Denny.

"Your partner wishes to partake," said the casino owner, who was by now so enamored of Cal he was willing to suffer the company of the ex-cop as well.

"He might be my partner but we're not Siamese twins," said Cal. "He can stay for the show." Cal stood suddenly and placed her napkin on the table. She had had enough.

"Careful," said Alex as Cal nearly bumped her head on the low-slung model of the solar system that hung directly over the table, bathing it in black light. It was clear the man would have liked to make Cal a part of his personal universe.

"You almost stuck your head in Uranus," said Denny, coming animatedly to life.

Cal ignored him. All night she'd had only one thought and that was to find Tony. It made her sick to think that as she ate her dinner, he might already have taken his life. It was true she wanted him to be part of her past, but on her terms, not his.

"Cal, please stay." Alex gave it one last try. He also looked ill at the thought of having Wickerstaff as his date for the rest of the evening. "We have comped rooms ready for you both."

Cal shook her head. "No, Alex, but thank you again." Tony's heavy ID bracelet jangled on her wrist. If Cal's motivations toward saving Tony were manipulative or selfish, she didn't know or care. Her pulse raced at the thought of Tony doing any form of violence to himself. She had to get out of there.

All at once, Denny jumped up as if he had a spring in his behind. He hit his head on the moons of Jupiter. Truly, Cal thought without any mercy, he was from another planet.

But how to get rid of this dirty-mouthed sleuth with his silvery alien eyes that watched her like a cat? Only when he was away could she play, she knew with desperation.

"Isn't that show rather risqué," she said to Alex in one last attempt to spark Denny's interest.

"We're all adults here, Cal," Alex winked at her, not having a clue as to her motivation.

"Seen one, seen 'em all," said Denny.

"Good night," Cal murmured to Alex, shaking his hand briefly. Denny followed her exit out the door like a shadow.

Night's cover wasn't any kinder to the Lucky Motel. The lights on the neon marquee lit it up like white powder on a whore's face. A fat yellow moon loomed obscenely over the building's second floor as raucous laughter and stiletto heels punctuated the evening's calm.

Cal unlocked her door. The fact that it was *her* door to *her* room made the act very unsettling. She circled the bed warily as if it were a coffin. Through the walls on one side came the sound of moaning as a bed thudded against the wall. From Denny's room came the sound of water pipes. Shower time!

Cal didn't hesitate; she ran for the door. The clear Reno night air spelled freedom. She pulled the motel door shut behind her, checked it once, and when she turned back around Denny was right there, in her face.

"Going for a stroll?" he said.

"A ride."

"Thought you were so tired." His eyes bored into her.

"Changed my mind," said Cal lightly, attempting a smile.

His face stretched at the mouth in a sort of rictus. The ability to clench these muscles was the strongest evidence thus far that the source of Denny's problems was not brain damage.

"Got to watch my little mice," he said.

"Mouse, singular," Cal corrected, wondering how this man could drink so much and still be on his feet. Wasn't there a level of alcohol that was toxic to the human body? Or was Denny Wickerstaff not human?

"Even a ride could be dangerous this time of night for a little lady."

"What's it to you, anyway?"

Denny gave her that cold, cold look she was coming to know so well. "I'm thinking maybe we're on our way to spend the night with Mr. T."

"What do you mean 'we'? Is that the investigatorial 'we'?"

"I'm thinkin' that maybe I should give you more credit for being smarter than you come across. That maybe you realize time is well spent getting tight with the big cheese."

"We were with him for three hours. Isn't that enough?"

"In the old-boy system you use every asset you got to get to what's really going down. What's shakin'. The inside—"

Cal cut him off; she was getting irritated with this parking-lot chitchat. "What inside? I don't follow."

"Find out what they're covering up. What really happened when that kid fell."

"Let me enlighten you, Denny." She nearly said "dummy." "The casino is our client."

"Better safe than sorry. When the truth be told, it'll be our butts on the line."

"So—"

"So, I was making sure you were doing your company duty. Watchin' you don't blow your big chance. Big-time."

"Making sure I'm on my way to the penthouse suite. Well, Denny, I hate to disappoint you, but I wasn't. I don't operate that way. I investigate, not fornicate." Cal surprised herself; that was a pretty good line for coming up on midnight in the parking lot of good and evil. "Also, being a detective doesn't mean everyone else is lying."

"*Everyone* is lying. And now I know your pansy-ass way of backing off from reality."

"So, what now? Are you going to ring up the big boys and rat me out?"

"Not yet, little mouse. I'm saving you for bigger and better." He turned and went back to his motel room, but he waited until she had gone into hers and closed the door.

Close to midnight Cal made her way back out to the parking lot, closing the rickety motel door behind her without a sound. She got to the car and quickly unlocked the Firebird's door; it was then she saw Wickerstaff asleep in the front passenger seat. Like a cat his eyes flicked open and met her stare.

Cal opened the car door and sat down in the driver's seat.

"Going somewhere?" he said.

"The room's too noisy and too stuffy."

"Try opening the window."

"The latch is stuck."

"I can fix it."

"Okay, here," she said, thrusting the room key at him. "Why are you following me?" she asked, tiring of the game.

"How can I follow you if you're not going anywhere?"

"I'm not in prison."

"I want to make sure you're not cutting deals on the side. Getting information I should be getting."

"You don't trust me, do you? And you want to be the superstar."

"I don't trust anyone, except myself," said Denny.

"That's really frightening, then, when you let yourself down."

"That's not going to happen."

"I wasn't going anywhere near the casino. Or Mr. T."

"Somehow I don't quite buy that," said Denny. "I'll go fix that window for you. And you really should get to bed, you need your sleep. Demanding job like this you want to at least last out the month."

Cal brushed her hair out of her eyes, Tony's ID bracelet making a solid jangling noise. "Is that a threat or a promise?" she said.

"Hey, I'm just a lowly peon like you," Denny protested.

"Okay, okay. I'll get to sleep after you fix the window. I'll wait out here till you're done."

"Now who doesn't trust who?" said Denny rhetorically.

"Who doesn't trust whom," Cal said. For a minute she toyed with the idea of just telling Denny about Tony. But Denny would somehow unearth how she had gotten into the credit card records. Denny was not a friend, he was a foe. And she had no right to offer up Orella. Sacrifice his career just to be able to unburden to Denny. Ex-L.A.P.D.— she could picture Carmen DeMille licking her lips.

"Oh, shit," he said, taking the key and getting out of the car. As soon as he unlocked the door to her motel room, Cal started the car and blasted out of the lot, laying at least twenty feet of rubber.

12

HER ADRENALINE WAS PUMPING, her hands were damp on the wheel. She was ready, ready or not. She had already gotten the address for Tony's motel from local information and memorized its location on a Reno street map. "Tony, Tony, Tony," she muttered as she drove, watching the rearview mirror for her blond nemesis, but there was nothing.

She laddered her way across town, making it even more difficult for someone to follow. She knew the moves in reverse having had them done to her during surveillances and now she did them, did all of them. She made constant right turns, she drove down alleys, she made unexpected U-turns. All clear.

The Four Aces Motel came into her anxious vision, a place so similar to the motel she was staying at she had a brief feeling she was back where she had started. A partying crowd on the second floor had spilled out of a room and onto the concrete walkway. If Tony was here, he wasn't getting much sleep. There were salutes of raised beer cans all around as Cal careened into the parking lot.

Actually, there were two entrances into the motel, since it was on a corner. Cal had to immediately veer into a parking space so as to avoid a car being driven by a dazed old Asian man. She also saw, in that split second, what appeared to be Tony's white boat of a Cadillac, its fins signaling like airplane rudders. The Caddy was stashed in a slot near the other exit.

Cal turned off the engine and thrust her car keys into her purse. She glanced back out at the Caddy and saw someone get into the driver's seat. The elderly Asian man had stopped his car and it was blocking Cal's. Cal grabbed her keys and hit the horn. All it did was make the old man jump. In the rearview mirror she could see the Caddy pulling out. Another second and it would be history.

She rolled down her window and shouted, which brought an answering echo from the second floor revelers. The Caddy was in the street. Cal pounded the steering wheel in frustration. The elderly driver slowly began to move. Cal started her car and backed out. It seemed to take forever but finally she, too, was at the exit. The Caddy was nowhere to be seen.

She turned left, the way the Caddy had headed. Up ahead, the streets were deserted; she hung a right back onto Virginia, the main drag. At the corner she looked both ways and was rewarded with the sight, one stoplight up, of the Caddy stopped at the red light. It turned green and with a screech, the car took off. So did Cal.

She hung back about a block. He wasn't turning around,

and it was too dark to see if he was checking his rearview mirror. Cal didn't want to get into a chase with him, not with his state of mind. She wanted to get him alone, calm him down, talk him down. Racing him would be like racing with the devil, he'd only get wilder and crazier.

As they headed out of town Cal began to have doubts. What if it wasn't even Tony driving? Maybe it wasn't his Caddy. Reno was known as a magnet for showy old cars. What if this was nothing more than a wild-goose chase?

The Caddy began to run red lights, slowing but then going through them. Cal was forced to do the same or lose him. If it was Tony, he was very messed up.

This was unfamiliar territory for Cal; she didn't know these streets. But she was relieved when the car finally pulled onto a highway on-ramp. Her relief, however, was short-lived as the Caddy accelerated to seventy, eighty, then ninety miles an hour. She began to worry.

The highway was a black ribbon threaded by moonlight and headlights. Cal didn't dare use her high beams. The shadowed countryside reeled by, sparse and desolate. A low mountain range stopped the vista from becoming infinite but its stony profile was not comforting. Cal rolled down the window an inch and heard a coyote howl. She felt like venting a bit herself.

Here she was, on a dark desert highway, following a man she had rejected. Actually, he had rejected her first in their early teen years after she wouldn't lose her virginity to him. He was now getting even all right, and it was happening at warp speed.

Cal could just see herself getting pulled over by the Nevada highway patrol. They had probably heard every line in the book except this one. "I'm following someone who I think is my old boyfriend. He's threatened to kill himself, Officer, and I'm doing this as a favor to his mother."

But there were no troopers around as mile after black mile rushed past, like the pages turning on a scary novel, a story she couldn't put down. She looked in the rearview mirror once or twice. Far behind her were headlights. The Caddy weaved a bit, claiming her full attention. She couldn't stop if she wanted to. She prayed to get off this road.

As if to give her some answers, the Caddy turned off abruptly, winging across three lanes of highway to an exit Cal never saw the name of. In the dark, she could only follow his lights. Now the road was two-lane but the combination of desert and mountain horizon seemed more up close and personal. There was no highway acting as a buffer.

Cal wondered if Tony, or whoever was driving, was trying to shake her. Did they know she was tailing them? They were making all the classic moves for shaking a pursuer. The road wound around the landscape like a picture drawn by a kindergartner with a fat black crayon.

She passed a closed convenience store with a lone gas pump. There wasn't a sound. The moon shone directly overhead, polished to the color of bone. The air smelled like earth. She found herself listening for the wail of the coyote.

As she came around a curve she almost passed a large square building squatting in the middle of nowhere. At the very last second her vision hung on the sight of the Caddy in the parking lot and she swung a hard right. Dust rose up in her headlights like a cloud of insects. There were quite a few cars parked all around, mostly a motley assortment of junkers. The Cadillac, though old, looked positively regal among this gathering.

Cal shut off her engine and the Firebird went silent after an abrupt shudder. On foot, she approached the structure, which didn't have a sign or a name or windows. Cal's hiking boots crunched in the gravel.

Maybe it was a topless place. A topless and bottomless place. She could handle that. Maybe it was a down and dirty local bar or gambling establishment. Lots of things were legal in Nevada and perhaps Tony was cheering up. A brothel? A witches' coven?

Cal opened the front door.

Tentatively she stepped inside but it was so dark she actually couldn't see. She stood still and realized she was in a small anteroom where evidently someone had forgotten to turn on a light or a bulb had burned out. Her eyes adjusted and she saw another door.

She opened it, and was met by a blast of cigarette smoke so intense she began to cough. The room was lit by flickering candles set up on round tables. Cal could see people talking in small clusters or standing by themselves, smoking fitfully. They looked at her without expression, their eyes seemingly sorrowful. This wasn't a very animated crowd, in fact, they looked like the sort of people you would find milling about in the front parlor of a funeral home. Cal moved farther into the room, looking for Tony, wondering why he had driven here.

Cal's eyes finally lit upon a white banner, one side of which was falling down. It seemed to read Welcome AA. Her hopes surged; perhaps Tony was here, seeking the support group he needed. But no Tony anywhere in sight.

She sat down at one of the round tables in the back of the room, keeping an eye on the men's room door. People had begun to filter down to their seats and the tables were getting filled up. A lanky tall man in his early thirties had taken a position underneath the banner. He held a microphone which buzzed with an earsplitting shriek that nobody seemed to notice except Cal.

"Okay, people, thank you for coming tonight, let's get this meeting under way. Good turnout. According to our latest survey, the group said they had a need for late-night meetings. So we're trying this out. First—any newcomers? You can stand and tell us anything you feel you'd like us to know about yourself."

"Is this affiliated with the regular Alcoholics Anonymous programs?" Cal asked a girl with a pale, emaciated face who was sitting next to her.

"No, not alcohol," said the girl strangely.

"What? I don't understand," said Cal.

"This is Narcotic Addicts Anonymous," said the girl in reply.

"Okay, we need some volunteers from the group." The man with the mike walked to where Cal sat and looked her straight in the eye. Cal felt as if she were at a nudist camp and was the only one there with clothes.

"The newcomer is the most important person here because we want to help. We can only keep what we have by giving back." Cal took the mike from him because it seemed as if he was not going to go away otherwise. "Tell us your name and why you're here."

The room grew hushed as Cal stood.

"I'm . . . Cal," she said, surprised at how weird her voice sounded in the quiet, "and I'm here"—she scanned the crowd, looking for Tony—"to . . ." Then she stopped. Somewhere in the recesses of her mind she'd hoped Tony would see her there and come forth. Kind of like a goofy scene out of a movie.

But then there was absolutely no way she could say another word. She just stood there, rendered speechless as she found herself looking straight into the gray wolflike eyes of Denny Wickerstaff.

She was transfixed as he held her steady gaze.

This time, she blinked first.

13

"SMACK? CRANK? ANGEL DUST? Freebase? I need you to tell me what you're on." Denny had his face right up into hers. His white teeth glinted in the neon glare of the Lucky Motel's sign like a night-prowling predator. He had followed her back to the motel in a dark brown compact car she had never seen before and had no idea how he got it, or who it belonged to. His eyes glowed with excitement.

Cal was in a quandary. She couldn't tell him she was looking for someone; he'd surely want to know who. Then he'd put two and two together and make five. Credit card records and phone trap lines were the only way to go. And then, somehow, she was certain, he'd follow the trail back to Orella. Denny *was* smart enough to find out about the credit card records. No search was untraceable. You just had to know where to look. There were federal regulations regarding these types of pretexts in gathering information. Even if Orella had run the pretexts from a pay phone, they were both still employees, on Worldwide's payroll.

Then would come the good part. Orella would go down, busted. No more Worldwide Investigations for either of them.

Maybe Denny would get the feds involved. She and Orella in the federal pen. Together at last. Dublin was minimum security, white-collar crime. Lompoc for the more hardened criminals. Denny would visit at Christmastime, his eyes glowing, bringing them a fruitcake, which of course is exactly what she was for getting involved.

But what choice did she really have? Sacrifice Tony because saving him meant crossing the line? She had made a choice and crossed that line. She had stretched the rules, chosen to ignore them, and finally she had broken them; her crime was attempting to save a human life because the bureaucracy wouldn't let her get involved. She'd be damned if she'd let that happen to Tony. He deserved another chance and was in no condition to make a decision that was so final, so devastating. Here we go again, zero tolerance.

"You're on it now, aren't you?" Denny was looking into her face as though she were a junkie. He was wearing a cologne that probably carried a zip code for its name. She was too exhausted to answer.

"You're in a bad way, Cal. You can tell me, trust me. I want to help." Denny was playing good cop, bad cop as a solo role. When he had been a cop Cal fervently hoped he always had chosen the bad-cop role. One look at those Ginsui knife eyes and anyone, in their right mind or not, would clam up.

"I'm not on drugs, Denny," she said simply.

"Why were you there?"

"I had taken a ride. I forgot my map. It was dark and that was the only place for miles. I had stopped to get directions."

As she spoke, she thought back to those last moments at the Narcotic Addicts Anonymous meeting. Had Tony seen her? Was he now tipped to her presence in Reno? Or what if, and you had to mightily believe in coincidence, that wasn't even his Cadillac. Or him driving; perhaps he had loaned the car to someone else. She relived the entire scene—

"Cal. Cal, I'm asking you a question." Denny, there in her face again. Unconsciousness was better.

"I didn't know what that place was." She sounded like a hardened criminal. Deny. Deny. "Where'd that car you're driving come from?" She wanted so badly for him to be on the defensive, instead of her.

"I had them drop off a rental car at the motel, just to be on the safe side. Know thy partner and all that commandment crap."

"You're good," Cal conceded, "you're very good at what you do." She thought of how he had tailed her successfully. Too successfully.

"Damn right," said Denny.

"Will you submit to drug testing when we return to San Francisco?" Denny uttered the words with a chilling zeal. It was then Cal realized she had been had. He had set her up, big-time. He had pegged her correctly from the start—a rule breaker. Only he had gotten her true crime wrong: caring about other people.

"Sure, I don't see why not," she'd call his bluff. Another federal pen came to mind: Terminal Island. She tried to recall what the federal uniform color was.

"These are sophisticated tests," Denny warned as if he had a legal obligation to do so. "They can pick up trace stuff from weeks prior."

"How trace? I mean, like is the test accurate?" Cal asked. She had taken some Advil. "I remember reading somewhere if you eat some type of vegetable it can mess up the results."

"I don't know nothing about any vegetables," Denny said sullenly.

"I wouldn't want it to pick up something that wasn't there."

"It'll pick up what needs to be picked up."

"Maybe I'll need a lawyer," Cal said, thinking of her mother. She had never thought she'd be glad her mother defended criminals, but right at this moment family connections could be very handy.

Denny sat abruptly back in his car seat. That was all he needed to know; all he needed to hear. No one ever asked for a lawyer unless they were guilty. And Cal was guilty of something; every fiber of his cop antenna told him that.

14

THE WHORES AT THE Lucky Motel had certainly gotten lucky; last night they had earned some major money. Judging by the newly evolved bags under Denny's eyes, he wasn't too thrilled by the ladies of the night plying their wares into the wee hours. He agreed, after a breakfast and black coffee, to take Mr. T. up on his offer, and within the hour they had transferred their luggage into rooms at the casino. Cal had to steel herself against letting her head spin with possible escape routes for the next evening as they made their way to the executive offices to conduct their first interview for the day.

Felicidad Hutton had the chiseled face of a Mayan princess and she carried herself with a regal bearing to match. Somehow Cal knew Denny wouldn't warm to this witness. And vice versa.

Felicidad sat very straight in her chair, eyes on Cal, but her tightly clenched hands betrayed her nerves. "We're going to tape," Cal said with a smile to put the woman at ease, "but anytime you want us to stop the recorder just give me a high sign." Cal made a time-out signal with her hands. "This isn't the Spanish Inquisition." Felicidad's eyes flashed with amusement and Cal knew her remarks were establishing rapport.

In the background, Denny paced, a tired scowl on his face. The witness looked over at him cautiously. Cal, frankly, was fed up with the good cop/bad cop routine.

"I need you to sign this," Cal said. "It means you are telling the truth." The woman signed on the two lines Cal indicated. "Ready?" Cal asked.

Felicidad nodded.

"This is Cal Brantley with Worldwide Investigations," she began, the word "investigations" sticking in her throat. It sounded so threatening. Yes, P. F. had been right. "Today is . . ." she went on, segueing into the standard introduction. Denny coughed and pointedly checked his watch. His expression said he would prefer smacking the woman around for the answers, instead of this polite groundwork.

"And I have your permission to record?" Cal was getting riled; Denny was making her lose her train of thought.

The witness nodded.

"You need to answer yes or no," Cal said gently. "The tape recorder won't pick up if you just nod." Felicidad gave a nervous laugh. Denny was getting to her too.

"Yes," she said softly, looking over at Denny. He glared at them both. Cal shut off the recorder.

"Denny, could you get us both some water? If you don't

mind?" She actually said the words that had formed as a plan. His mouth dropped open a full inch. It was like asking Nixon if he had any new cassette tapes on him.

Denny stomped out of the room, closing the door with a bit more force than was required.

"Don't mind him," Cal leaned forward as if sharing a great secret, "he was up late last night."

"The casino life, some people can't get used to it," the witness responded.

"Men. They always overdo things," said Cal.

"This is a truth," said Felicidad.

Cal began the recorder again, smoothly getting some personal data from the witness. "In case I need to get hold of you, and you're not working here anymore or your home phone is disconnected, is there someone, a friend or relative, who would know where you are?"

"My sister?"

"Yes, that would be fine," said Cal.

The witness gave the phone number.

"Let's talk about what happened that day, September sixth, in the casino. What time had you reported for work?"

"I had gotten on at one."

"A.M. or P.M.?"

"One P.M."

"You're a blackjack dealer?"

The witness nodded, then remembered, and said "Yes" directly into the recorder.

"How long have you worked at the casino?"

"Six months."

"And prior to that, where did you work?"

"The Nugget."

"Blackjack dealer?"

"Yes."

"And why did you leave there?"

"I like my shift here better. There, at the Nugget, I worked swing. I couldn't see my husband at all. He works graveyard at his job. We have time together now."

"Any kids?"

"Two, a boy and a girl."

"Great. What are their ages?"

"Marissa is ten. Alejandro is seven."

"You don't look old enough to have a ten-year-old," Cal exclaimed honestly.

The witness smiled just as Denny came back into the room. He held out the two cups of water as if he had gone to the well to get it. He placed the drinks on the table and when they didn't make immediate moves towards drinking, he scowled. Cal and Felicidad both ignored him.

"About what time did the accident happen?" Cal asked.

"It was about four-fifteen. I had just returned from a break."

"A smoke break?" Cal asked curiously.

"You don't want to smoke cigarettes after you've been in the casino all day," Felicidad answered. "I went outside and took a walk."

"Tell me, in your own words, what you saw. Take it from the beginning, and I'll throw in questions as I need to."

"Well . . ." Here Felicidad looked down at a button on

her vest. "I was pretty much into my table. There's always lots of noise in the casino. Little shouts, yells, men's, women's voices. Sometimes laughter. You know. It's all going through my head like background. Well, anyway, that day, I catch sight of this little boy going down the escalator. The way he is looking at everything. He catches my attention. I like children. I look up and next thing I see, this boy falls." The witness paused. Cal waited, gave her an encouraging nod and asked, "How did he fall?"

"It happened so fast, I don't know. An accident. He tripped and fell. I couldn't see at that point because the side of the escalator blocked my view."

"I can see by this floor plan, you were at an angle." Cal felt she needed to say something. The woman looked as if she were going to break down.

"Yes, there are no tables in the aisle."

"How many feet do you think you were from the escalator?"

"Twenty? Thirty?"

"Pretty close," Cal remarked sympathetically. "Did anyone push the boy? Any other kids, perhaps? You know, horseplay?"

"No other kids that I could see. A very large woman was in the front of him. I think, maybe, it was the boy's mother."

"In front of him?" Cal was trying to get this straight.

"Front, yes."

"And the child was four years old." Cal shook her head. "And no one was holding on to him?"

"There was that woman in back of him. But holding him, no. They looked to be on separate steps."

"There's that sign on the escalator," Cal said, " 'please hold children by the hand.' "

"Also, there was the stroller."

"The stroller. Isn't a four-year-old a little old for a stroller?" asked Cal.

"Kids that age get tired," said Felicidad. "And they're too big to carry for any period of time."

"Tell me more about the stroller."

"The large blond. The one in front of the boy. She had the stroller. Not folded up, either. Maybe there was another child in there," said Felicidad, her eyes now wide with the memory.

"No strollers allowed on those escalators," said Cal.

"No," the witness agreed.

"Then what did you see?"

"Well, the escalator was very crowded. It was like a traffic jam."

"Then what happened?" Cal prompted.

"There was more yelling. Many people—a crowd—formed at the base of the escalator. I see Mr. LaSchiaffa standing there. He looks very angry. But he doesn't make any motion towards the boy. Maybe he doesn't see the boy. I can't see the boy. A man comes then with a knife."

"Mr. LaSchiaffa—he's the pit boss?" asks Cal. "Your direct supervisor?"

"Yes."

"Tell me more about the knife," said Cal.

"A big knife. This man is holding it out, like this." The witness motioned. "A hunting knife maybe, not like your knife you use in the kitchen. Later, I hear the boy's jacket got stuck."

"The blond woman, the one that possibly is the mother. Tell me more about her actions, what she did," asked Cal.

"She didn't do anything. She just stood there. And the other lady, a Filipina maybe, the one I thought was in the back of the boy. Now I think, maybe she is not with them. I see her in the back of the crowd."

"You think she was Filipino though?"

"My mother, she is from Manila. That's how I noticed."

"And that blond lady. She didn't try to get the boy's jacket free?"

"Not that I could see. Maybe she's not even the mother. Then I see them take the boy out, on a stretcher."

There was silence in the room. The tape spun, slowly. Even Denny had stopped pacing. "Did you know any of these people?" he put in.

"No, I never saw them before."

"Never in the casino?"

"No. Never."

"How about the guy with the knife?"

Felicidad thought for a long moment. "Him, yeah. I've seen him before in the casino. He never plays my table. I've seen him play the video poker."

"Why does he stand out in your mind?" asked Cal. "Other than the knife, I mean."

131

"I've seen him with this lady. All in black leather with tattoos on her. She's old, sixty maybe."

"Hard to forget," Cal agreed. "A day you won't forget." Felicidad nodded.

"Not to mention the murder of the cocktail waitress," Cal added.

"I didn't even know her. I heard it was only her second day working at the casino."

"Anything else that comes to mind?" asked Cal. Felicidad shook her head, forgetting the rule about verbally answering. Cal didn't prompt her.

"He was about the age of my son," Felicidad said sadly. Denny was standing directly in back of her. He shook his head and motioned toward the door.

Cal ended the statement by asking on tape if the witness knew she was being recorded and if Cal had permission to record. When Felicidad left the room, Cal and Denny looked at each other.

"The mother took the stroller on the escalator," Cal said in a low tone.

"So what?"

"Seems to me like the stroller could have been the proximate cause of the entire accident. There's comparative negligence on her then."

"No jury would take her money away from her," said Denny coldly.

"Why are you so set on giving this woman everything?" said Cal.

"Why are you so set on taking it away?" Denny retorted.

"I'm not set on taking it away," Cal replied. "But that's the way this system works. We work for the casino, for the insurance carrier. If we can uncover some information that gives us a bargaining edge, so be it."

"It stinks," said Denny. "Just give the mother her money."

"Maybe as a police officer you saw little kids as the final innocent victims, Denny, but we have to separate ourselves out from that. A little kid, four years old, what did he do to deserve this terrible fate, you think? But listen—he was with his parent. And parents have a duty to take care of their children. I wonder why she was in front of him?" Cal mused.

Denny had his wallet out. "This is my kid," he said, handing over a picture to Cal. "This is my future."

Cal stared down at a child of about eight who bore absolutely no resemblance to Denny.

"Looks like his mother," said Denny, reading her mind as usual. "My ex-wife."

"Cute kid," said Cal, seeing for the first time an entire new side of Denny. He looked shy, calm, almost serene.

"I'd kill for that kid," said Denny, coming quickly back to form.

"I bet you would," replied Cal.

The next four witnesses gave similar versions of Felicidad's testimony. She, however, had not only been the nearest to the accident site but the most observant. One other person, an employee whose job was going around with a cart making change, said that the woman in back of the boy had been carrying what looked like a tote or a diaper bag.

"For a four-year-old?" Cal said to Denny when the witness had left.

"Boys can be difficult to potty train," said Denny with his usual candor. Cal found herself thinking that there might be a link between the two women, or—and this gave Cal pause—the Filipino woman might be a very important witness.

They broke for lunch and got ready for their interview with the pit boss LaSchiaffa, and his lawyer at three o'clock.

The sight of the attorney's nameplate on the door seemed to send Denny into a spin. Cal knew immediately he was going to be one of those people who are at their worst around lawyers. Since she had grown up around one, it didn't faze her in the least, and she played this as an asset.

The lawyer was a woman and this didn't help matters. She came out to greet them in the reception area. She was wearing a very short skirt with opaque black hosiery. The outfit was calculated to have an effect on everyone: other attorneys, other women, and judges. Denny eyed her skirt hem as if it were Pandora's box.

"How long will this take, people?" she asked, checking her Rolex.

Cal felt as though she had just gotten into a cab and the flag went up. "An hour," Cal answered. "If we have no interruptions," she added sweetly.

"We have a stress claim going, if you catch my drift," said the attorney.

"Drift?" said Denny.

"My client might exhibit a tendency to get a bit carried away." She turned to Cal. The lawyer's eyes locked with hers and in a split second they understood each other. The lawyer led them into the conference room, where she introduced her client.

"Denny," said Cal, and he literally jumped, startled, "are you going to do the honors?"

"Honors?"

"Are you going to take the statement? We're ready to go." It was worth it, deferring to him.

Denny looked at the pit boss, Justin LaSchiaffa, who had already begun to perspire. Then he looked at the attorney's legs. "Go for it, Cal. You need the practice."

"Denny's joking, of course, I've got a few more years of experience in the insurance industry than he does."

"But I've questioned more people than you," said Denny, picking an incredibly bad time to get into a pissing match with her. He grinned at her evilly. She smiled back as if he were the butt of a secret joke.

"Okay, I'll question Mr. LaSchiaffa. But Denny, please, at the end, feel free to ask anything you feel is pertinent. If, of course, I've left anything out." Cal vowed to cover every base. "I'd like to tape," she said to the attorney.

"Of course, we'd like a transcript."

"Certainly."

Cal began the tape recorder and asked the preliminary questions, hoping that the witness would last through the entire thing.

"Justin—may I call you Justin? You haven't worked since the accident?"

"Yes."

"We won't get into any questions that touch on your pending workers' comp case," Cal assured him, but knew she wouldn't have to worry about getting into foul territory; the attorney would see to that. "Why don't you tell me in your own words what happened that afternoon? The day of the accident?"

"I really don't remember."

Denny gave Cal a look that said, Hey, we're going to get off early. Cal ignored him and instead looked questioningly at the attorney, who was picking lint off her stocking.

"Just answer the best you can," she said to her client without looking up.

"I don't recall."

"Does Mr. LaSchiaffa have amnesia?" Cal directed this query at the attorney.

"Post-traumatic stress disorder," she said in a clipped manner that was so devoid of feeling you could almost hear the dollar signs clinking on the cash register in the sky.

Cal mentally threw her hands up in the air. They were going to stonewall the liability investigation for the sake of LaSchiaffa's cash cow: his workers' comp case. That is, unless Cal could jar him loose.

"Mr. LaSchiaffa, are you under any medication?" Cal asked.

"Now?"

"Yes, at the time of this recorded statement?"

The witness looked at his attorney. All sympathy Cal might have had for him went out the window.

The attorney nodded at her client and he finally answered. "Yes, I'm on Prozac."

"Anything else?"

"I have an inhaler, for my asthma."

"Do you feel that any of these medications prevent you from remembering the answers to my questions?"

He looked at his attorney and she shook her head. "No."

"When did you last take any medication?"

"I took my Prozac this morning."

"As I understand it, in post-traumatic stress disorder, it's actually beneficial for the person to try and relive the events that have triggered their current stress. I know we're not in a regular psychotherapy setting, but with your attorney's permission, why don't we give it a try?"

"Sure," said the attorney.

"We'll take it slow," Cal assured the pit boss.

"Is that someone at the door?" LaSchiaffa suddenly stood up.

"Probably it's only my secretary," the attorney said.

Denny shook his head and tapped his fingers against his pants leg. "You can sit down, buddy," he said.

"Sit down, Justin," said the attorney.

After one more long look at the door, he did.

"Ready to go on?" Cal asked.

He nodded slowly.

"Okay. What time did you get to work that day?"

"I started at one o'clock."

"Did anything happen that was unusual on the way to work or was this a normal day?"

"Everything was normal."

"When did you first notice something was wrong?"

"Wrong?"

"Yes. What did you see or hear?"

"I heard . . . I saw . . ." The witness gulped, choked, then began to cough.

"Jesus, I'll get the water," said Denny. "Where is it?" he asked the attorney who looked at him blankly. "Water?" he raised his voice.

"Oh, outside," said the attorney.

Denny was back in two seconds as if this were a show he didn't want to miss. The witness was perspiring heavily and he mopped at his face with a dirty-looking handkerchief.

"Let's try that last question again. Just tell me what drew your attention to the escalator. Was it something you heard? Or saw?" Cal gave LaSchiaffa a brief smile.

The witness seemed to gather all his strength. "I saw this large woman coming down the escalator with a stroller. It caught my eye because strollers are not allowed on the escalator. I rushed over to tell her not to do that again. But before I even got there—before I could reach her—the stroller bumped against her like she had forgotten it was there. She stumbled. Then—then—I don't, I don't know—"

"Okay," said Cal. "You're doing great. Just tell me what

happened next." Evidently he hadn't seen the boy in back of the woman.

"I don't—"

"Try."

"This other woman lost her balance. Yes, she started to fall. Then people on the escalator were screaming. Screaming." LaSchiaffa covered his ears.

"When did you first see the boy?"

"The boy—" It came out as a squeak. Then the witness fell silent. Cal didn't say anything either. "I didn't see him at first," he said with a shudder.

"Can you describe the boy for me," Cal tried to keep him talking.

"He was a small child."

"Small, you mean short?"

"No, just young. Fairly young. I'm not good at kid's ages."

"Four, five years old?"

LaSchiaffa nodded. "The kid was down there, all the way on the last escalator stair. That's why I didn't see him. I tried to get to him but the blond woman wouldn't move."

"She wouldn't let you help him?"

"She didn't stop me, she was just so big. And she just stood there."

"Did you realize the boy was stuck?"

"No. Not at first."

"Go on."

"I thought he had just fallen. There was another woman

who lost her balance in back of him. She didn't fall, though."

"Can you describe this woman?"

"She was young. She seemed upset. I saw the side of her face, she had a big black birthmark here." The pit boss put his finger up beside his eye.

"How did the woman appear upset?" Cal wanted to keep him going.

"She made a sound, like a wail."

"Was she Caucasian?"

"Cauc—?"

"White," said his attorney sharply. "Was she white?"

"No. Now that you ask. No, I don't think so."

"Was she carrying anything?" asked Cal.

"I don't—I can't—"

"Did you, at any time, see anyone holding the boy by the hand?"

"The big woman, the blond, she was by herself, all by herself on a separate step. I didn't see the boy until—until—" LaSchiaffa covered his face with his hands. Cal paused and looked over at Denny, who was shaking his head in disgust.

"Let me get this straight." Denny suddenly stood up. "You didn't see the kid?"

"I saw—I saw the stroller." The witness's head snapped up, his eyes guarded.

"When did you first realize there an accident?" Denny said sharply.

"This man. He came running at me, at us, with a knife."

"You're losing me, fella."

"Denny, I think I'll—" Cal tried to regain control of the

interview. Denny gave her an impatient wave.

"It all happened—" said LaSchiaffa.

"Let's take it from the top." Denny cut the witness off. "You see the stroller. The blond stumbles. The guy runs at you with a knife—"

"No. Not at me. He's running—"

"Yeah, yeah." Denny got up and sat down in a chair nearer to LaSchiaffa. His eyes were cold and unyielding. "Okay, then what?" Denny was not giving the witness a chance to get into his prior protestations of not recalling. Cal had to admit that, at some level, it was working.

"Someone told me after that I had hit the emergency button. I don't recall—"

"Let's take it slower, buddy. You need to tell us what went down," said Denny. "Now, you hit the emergency button and then this guy comes running?"

"I don't—"

"You're telling me you didn't hit the button." Denny was baiting him. The lawyer didn't say a word.

"I hit the button, then this guy came running with the knife."

"But you didn't see the kid?"

"I told her—I told her not to bring the stroller on—"

"It's clear to me that the jacket got stuck after you pressed the button," said Denny.

"After I pressed—" The witness stood, swaying. "I didn't—"

"No," Cal stood, "he's not saying you—"

"I didn't see the kid! I didn't see him!" The witness was

starting to shout. "I didn't make him fall down. He was down. He was stuck before I pressed the stop button. I didn't kill him! I didn't kill him!" the witness screamed.

"You—you—" Denny stood.

"Denny, I think we got enough," said Cal in the understatement of the year.

"I think we're getting more into the workers' comp arena now," said the attorney. She was the only one still seated.

"We've taken our best shot," agreed Denny, looking as though he had broken a murder suspect into confessing.

"I pressed the button," LaSchiaffa said to no one in particular. "I pressed the button!" He grabbed his hair and pulled it in distress. At this point Cal didn't know if it was feigned or not.

Denny started to walk toward the door. LaSchiaffa ran toward him and reached for Denny's shoulder. Denny held out his hand and firmly got LaSchiaffa by the forearm. "Hey, dude, cool it," said Denny. "Pull yourself together, man."

"I pressed the button!" LaSchiaffa shrieked.

Denny hustled through the door, Cal at his heels.

15

TONY WAS GONE, LIKE the wind. Cal had used all her persuasive powers to get the desk clerk to check his register.

"Saw that big boat of a Caddy pull outta here, right about noon," said the clerk. "Checkout's noon."

"Do you recall if he mentioned where he was heading?" Cal asked.

The clerk scratched his sparse goatee. "They just come and they go. Come and go."

"Did he seem upset?" Cal asked.

"*I'd* be upset if I had missed you," he said. "I get off in about twenty minutes you want to catch some dinner."

"I'll have to pass," said Cal, "I have to do some work."

"All work and no play," warned the clerk.

"Thanks, I'll remember that," said Cal.

Denny had been bellied up to the bar when she had last seen him, but that was no guarantee he wasn't tailing her. She found a pay phone, feeling all the while increasingly nervous.

Her head had a tight feeling above her eyebrows as though a major headache was a definite possibility. She never got headaches, but life had never been quite like this before.

She had visions of Tony hanging by the throat in some dingy motel bathroom. Tony with a gun to his temple. Tony swimming in blood. How would she break the news of her failure to Mrs. Lazio? And she did consider it her own personal defeat. For, when all was said and done, it would only be by her own ineffectiveness that Tony had succeeded. She was certain she could stop him, if only she could get to him.

She found a pay phone and called Glendale. Orella came on almost immediately; he was still at the office.

"Cal! Did you find him?" Orella's voice was a low sexy rumble.

"I was on him last night. At least I think it was him. I never got close enough to see who was driving."

"So you didn't connect?"

"Connect." Cal felt as if she were going to break into hysterical laughter. "I ended up in the boondocks at some meeting of Narcotic Addicts Anonymous. Tony was nowhere in sight. And to make matters worse, that ex-cop Wickerstaff had followed me. Now he thinks I'm some kind of junkie."

"That Wickerstaff is bad news. I heard some talk about him. He killed another cop."

"He told me about somebody he killed in a bar fight. But he didn't say it was another cop."

"I heard the story in the break room. It was a cop bar. That's one crazy dude, Cal."

"I need some more credit card info," she said, trying to keep her voice from wavering. A headache was starting and she winced with the force of it.

"Too late today. You realize what a chance we're taking, each time we get into that system?"

"This goes beyond rules. Beyond the law. A man's life could be in the balance."

"I thought the guy was a jerk. He wants to off himself that's his own business."

"Not if I can help it," said Cal firmly.

"I'll do it to help you, Cal. Not for that asshole's, excuse me, sake. Things are closed up tight for tonight. I can get on it first thing in the morning. I take it that he's checked out of where he was?"

"Long gone," said Cal wearily. "I did statements with Wickerstaff all day. No way could I make contact with Tony. They didn't even have telephones in the rooms in the motel he was staying at. I'll never forgive myself, Orella—"

"Okay, okay. I said I'd help. Wait one sec, where is that paper . . . here, okay. There was one more credit card entry along with the motel one. Just thought you wouldn't need it."

"What? What?" Cal forgot her headache.

"The Old Players Club, Douglas Alley. Guy's a big spender—thirty-five dollars."

"In Reno?"

"Yeah, Reno," said Orella. "Where's Wickerstaff now?" he said with a trace of caution coming into his tone.

"He had me drop him off at the casino. I went up to the

room and when I left I saw him having a drink. I called in this morning to tell the office we're staying at the casino now."

"Do you think he followed you again?" Orella asked worriedly.

"So he sees me making a phone call. So sue me. Tony is more important than this job."

"There's more riding on this than the job, Cal," Orella flatly pointed out. "Our new job could be in a prison laundry."

"I'll watch out for him," Cal promised.

"Be cool," said Orella.

"I'm cool," Cal said, thanking him and promising to call first chance she got in the morning. A bead of sweat rolled down the side of her face and plopped on the phone booth shelf.

Douglas Alley smelled like an alley.

It stank of rotting food and car exhaust fumes and something pretty close to indescribable that got a person thinking of the endless food chain. Things a person in their right mind didn't want to think of if they could at all help it.

Cal sat at the nickel video poker machine for two hours at the Old Players Club. Then she switched to another machine two stools down. She found herself talking to the new machine, reasoning with it, asking it questions. When she found herself praying to it she knew she had had enough. It was close to midnight and Tony hadn't showed.

Maybe he had left town; maybe he had left the planet.

Cal had given it a shot.

Bad choice of words.

She was getting rummy even though she had been drinking Virgin Mary's. Her hands were as black as if she had been cleaning chimneys. Money was, in truth, dirty. She gathered her purse by the strap and set off for the ladies' room.

The club wasn't very large but apparently had been even smaller at one time. A long hallway connected the room she had been in with another. This room was smaller with only one-armed bandits and no gaming tables. There was a lone bartender on duty and a snack bar that was closed. About fifteen people were there, engrossed in their machines. Cal hoped Tony hadn't been in this other room while she had been at her own machine. She *was* getting rummy.

The rest rooms were off the side of the snack bar. A young couple in their late teens were perched on one of the chairs at a table. The girl straddled the boy face-forward. No one was paying them any mind, including the bartender, who continued wiping down the bar. Cal pushed open the door to the ladies' room with the side of her dirty hand. She went inside and started to scrub. It took two washings before the pink of her skin was clear again. Then she went into the stall. Her neck and back ached.

She had turned to bolt the door latch when she heard a noise. Maybe it was because of Denny but her hearing was more sensitive than usual. She paused as the outside door to the ladies' room opened. The door to the stall she was in was pushed open an inch. She'd file for work comp stress; she'd had enough of this Denny. Bad person to take on, but he'd pushed too far, she was thinking as the door smashed open. The teenager who had been sitting astride her boyfriend came flying at her. Cal felt the girl's fingers go for her throat as out of the corner of her vision she saw the girl eye her purse, which was hanging from a metal bar in the stall.

The girl's face was right in hers, sharp nails digging into her skin as she struggled to get a firmer grip on Cal's neck. Cal spat in her face and for a moment the fingers slackened, the hold loosened. Cal kicked her in the knee with one of her hiking boots and heard a grunt of pain in response. She remembered growing up and tussling with her cousin Gigi. Gigi could kick like a mule. Those experiences had fine-tuned Cal's fighting skills. It was either that or be black-and-blue.

The girl came at Cal again. There was no shortcut out of this encounter. The girl smelled unwashed and her acrid stink made Cal all the more alert. She was pinned in back of the toilet, which actually smelled better than the girl. She struggled to get another kick in but the stall was too confining. She pushed the girl with all her strength and wished she hadn't been hurt in that car accident. All her strength wasn't going to be good enough tonight.

Then she had a sudden recall of that video Laurie had made her watch, the video Linda had given her. Chuck Norris saying that the main thing was *to get away from an encounter.* Get away, that would be a good thing.

The girl sprang at her again like a jungle animal. Cal made a fist and let fly, angling her hand like Chuck's in the video. She didn't want to break any of her own bones. She felt it connect with the girl's cheek. The teenager's eyes were so wild the punch didn't slow her, but Cal's second one did. The smashing hand.

She remembered Laurie standing in her living room saying "break and smash" over and over. At least she'd live and buy her friend some lunch. The smashing hand crashed into the teenager's nose. Blood spurted out as the teenage attacker yelped, crashing backward and slamming the door to the stall back open. Right behind her was her boyfriend.

Cal didn't hesitate. She was not going to go down in the Old Players Club. She whipped at him with the buckle on the strap of her handbag. He grabbed at his eyes and stumbled backward out into the hallway. Cal heard several muffled thuds from that direction and she went toward the door. A hand reached for her ankle and she looked down at the teenage girl, who hadn't had enough. Well, Cal had.

She smashed at the hand with her boot, feeling disgust at having to inflict pain, but knowing she had to when it was her own survival at stake. There was no resistance this time as she got to the door.

Outside, the boy was down on the floor, unmoving.

Cal picked her way around him cautiously but quickly. She wondered why he was out cold. Had she hit him that hard with her handbag strap? She hadn't thought she did. Maybe he had just passed out from too many drugs. She reached the end of the short hallway and the relative safety of the interior of the Old Players Club.

Evidently nobody had heard the attack. A football game was playing on the TV above the bar and the sound was very loud. The bartender still rubbed at the bar with his rag and the same players sat at their machines. The same old players.

Cal quickly went out the exit and there, in the darkened alley, was terribly sick.

16

SPARKS, NEVADA, WAS AS dull as a place could get, with small dun-colored block houses, postage-stamp-sized lawns, and cheap landscaping. A corner house had three red rose bushes and they were the most colorful spot for a mile.

"You look like shit," said Denny as he drove. He always drove now when they went anywhere.

Cal didn't say a word; instead she concentrated on checking for the address they needed. "Next block," she cautioned him.

"Nag, nag," he said, baiting her. Why was he baiting her when she was ready to get into a somewhat normal working relationship with him?

"Circle the block once, circle," she commanded. There was a red car with a white convertible top in the driveway.

"Circle, circle," he complained. "You always act like you're in a murder mystery. We're just going to meet with the dead kid's mom, for chrissake."

"I always like to check out situations," Cal responded.

"But this ain't a situation," Denny whined. "Now, there's a funny vanity plate. Or I wonder if they just happened to pull a corker like that by luck of the draw."

"What plate?" Cal asked.

"That red car in the driveway of our ex-mom. It said 1HOELE. Get it?"

"Sure, Denny, sure. Whatever turns you on," said Cal in a monotone. He would not get to her today, no matter what.

"So what do you think? Is it okay to make our stop? No ax murderers lying in wait?"

"It's cool," said Cal in her new you're-not-getting-to-me voice.

"Poor old mom. Can you imagine having your kid killed right in front of your eyes? Visitor's car is gone. Or else mom took off without waiting for us," Denny remarked as he parked the car.

"Ding-dong," he said happily as he rang the bell. Cal wondered why he was in such a good mood today. Was it because she was in such a cruddy one?

The door swung open and even Denny had to look up. This woman was tall. Tall and solid. She looked at Denny as though if she hadn't eaten breakfast, he could be fodder.

"Denny Wickerstaff, Mrs. ah, um, Fanny. We have an appointment."

The giant stood aside silently to let them both inside. Cal introduced herself as she went by. The woman made absolutely no acknowledgment. Other than the movement to let them into the house, she might have been a cigar store Indian.

The furniture was nondescript Sears Roebuck stuff. It looked fairly new but for the places where the big woman had sat. She had left her mark in the form of craters. There wasn't a trace of a child anywhere, if there had been before. No toys, no little shoes, no plastic drinking cups. Cal thought of the jacket. The jacket without a label.

"Mrs. Fanny, we're here to help expedite the handling of your claim," Cal said, trying to ease the tension that had filled the room. "We realize this is a terrible time for you, and we apologize, but we're here in town now. If you feel we need to postpone, we can put this off till some other time."

"Ask your questions and be done with it," said Violetta Fanny in a rumbling voice. Cal thought the woman could record herself for tapes at Halloween and make a bundle. She tried to feel sorry for her but couldn't bring herself to that emotion. There was an aura about her, in addition to her appearance.

Cal looked at her more closely and found that the more she looked the weirder the woman appeared.

Her eyes, for instance. One was blue and one was brown.

Her face was crisscrossed with dozens of straight scars. Golden blond hair framed this face, hair the color movie stars had favored in the forties. The woman's hands and feet were enormous.

Denny sat down and pulled out his notepad. Cal noticed he had avoided sitting in any craters. She followed suit. With an audible whoosh of air, so did the big blond; she, however settled in a crater.

"We'd like to start, Mrs. Fanny, by saying we're sorry about your son," Denny said, ex-L.A.P.D. Prince Charming.

The woman nodded. She stared hard at Denny with her blue eye; the brown one wandered in its gaze around the living room. Cal hoped the eye wouldn't light on her. Her immediate aversion to the woman was odd and disturbing.

". . . and we need to go over a couple of basic things . . ." Denny was saying. Cal forced herself to pay attention. "Is this your permanent address?"

Violetta seemed to consider the question a bit too long. "Yes, but I've still got some property up in Virginia City."

"And the boy's father . . . is he? . . ." Denny wasn't any good at subtlety. Hellfire flamed on the woman's face, but Denny didn't seem to notice.

"There is no father," said the woman.

"We ask this because we need to be legally certain when we settle the claim," Denny said.

"You can make the check out to me," Voiletta said.

Sure, said Cal's inner missile-tracking system.

"We need a copy of the death certificate," said Denny.

"I can get you one of those."

"Oh, and one of the boy's birth certificate," said Cal casually, without looking up from her notepad.

"I can get them both for you right now," said Violetta, and walked ponderously to another room.

"Birth certificate?" Denny hissed.

"Humor me," said Cal.

Violetta was back quickly as if she kept death certificates

readily handy. Cal let Denny take them from her; the less the woman noticed her, the better.

"Can you tell us about that day?" asked Denny.

"That day?"

"The day of the accident."

"That day. The day the boy died," the woman intoned strangely. Was she in shock, Cal wondered. Medicated?

"Mrs. Fanny, have you taken any medication in the last twenty-four hours? And Denny, shouldn't you be taping? Remember the new company rule?" Cal whipped out her tape recorder and placed it on the table in front of Denny and Violetta.

"I don't do drugs," said Violetta for the record.

"By the way," Cal said for the recorder's benefit, "we're here with Mrs. Violetta Fanny in Sparks, Nevada. Mrs. Fanny, do we have permission to record you?"

Violetta said yes, and Cal finished the introductions for taping.

"So," said Denny, as if keeping himself on track, "let's talk about that day."

"We were going back home and almost out the casino door," said the woman.

"You say 'we.' Who exactly was in your party?" asked Denny.

"Party? What party?"

"Who was with you?"

"Why, just me. Me and my boy."

"Go on."

"Not much more to go on. Boy was killed by your casino's escalator, that's what happened."

"You had a stroller on the escalator, Mrs. Fanny?" asked Denny haltingly.

"So what about it?" the woman challenged him.

"All I asked was if you had a stroller."

"Couldn't find the elevator," she said as if that solved that aspect.

"Where were you standing when this all—" Denny started to continue but the woman cut him off.

"Where was I standing?" she raised her voice to a boom and lurched to her feet. "My boy was kilt by your escalator. And you ask me where I was standing? Where were you standing? My boy, all that I have in this world. Taken from me. Gone. Something was wrong with that escalator, as sure as I stand here, it was defective. It kilt my boy. You should have seen his face—swollen, blue. His tongue hangin' like a dog's. Dead! Kilt on the spot." She paused for breath and Denny sprang to his feet.

"We didn't mean to upset you Mrs., ah, Miss Fanny."

"Upset me. You didn't mean—Get out. Get the damn hell out of my house! You did it. Your escalator. You kilt my—"

Cal didn't hear any more; she'd had enough. She left and got inside the car quickly. Denny soon followed as the front door crashed behind him. He got in the car and flung the certificates into Cal's lap.

"Jesus," he said, and put the car into gear. Cal didn't look back even once at the giantess's lair.

17

"DID I EVER TELL you about the time I was off duty and I saw this woman being dragged into a car?" Denny was driving, one forearm draped casually over the steering wheel. Cal didn't answer; she was replaying the scene at the house over and over in her mind.

"Well, I'm on Sunset, see, and I look down this side street. There's this woman, absolutely no top on, nothin'. Good-looking woman, too. She's being dragged into this car with two guys. I yell at 'em to stop, see, and they keep on doin' what they're doin'. She's screaming like you wouldn't believe.

"They got her in the car now and take off a ways down the street. It's at night, so traffic was lighter and I'm after 'em. They're driving wild, must have been drunk. Maybe she was drunk, too. I don't know. Well, anyway, they take this right turn, see. Only thing is, it's a dead end. I shot them both. Dead. That woman was one grateful bitch. I tell you.

Good-looking woman, too." Denny's eyes were that dead gray now; he spoke in a flat tone.

"You handled things just fine back there," Cal said.

"Am I talking about that now?"

"Well, I was attempting to make a connection between the two events," Cal said.

"What the hell does one have to do with the other?" Denny's face darkened. He smoothed his already perfect hair with his hand.

Because this last thing didn't turn out like you planned, Cal was thinking. *And the woman wasn't good-looking.*

"Man, she was rough around the edges," Denny commented.

"Grieving mother," Cal said thoughtfully.

"A big grieving mother," said Denny.

"Did you notice," said Cal, "that she had no pictures of the boy anywhere?"

"Maybe she can't bear to see them," said Denny. "But I handled her okay. She was just falling apart on her own."

"She'll probably get an attorney now," said Cal.

"And you're saying that's my fault?" Denny swung a hard right with the wheel.

"I'm not saying anything's your fault."

"But you're going to spread the word I blew it."

"Not at all."

"Don't hand me that crap. You've got that holier-than-thou attitude."

"No, that's not true," said Cal.

"Not true, my fuckin' ass. You're full of shit."

"I do believe you've used up your yearly allotment of swear words," Cal said, suddenly having her fill of Denny's dirty mouth.

"My allotment. Well, fuck you. You just sat there in that living room like the cat that fucked the canary. You let that woman fuck me." Denny was agitated now and he was needling Cal the only way he knew would get to her.

"You just sat there," Denny went on, gathering steam, "looking like shit. You been up all night or what? Talk about having your wits about you, witless is more like it."

Cal's back ached and her head throbbed. She pressed a hand to her temple.

"You outta dope or what?" Denny snarled. "You comin' down,'cause you certainly look down to me. A lotta help you were back there. You coulda handled her. Woman to woman, and all that shit. Now the case is fucked. I'm fucked and you're fucked. We'll both take the fuckin' heat on this one, I promise." A small piece of spittle flew from Denny's lips.

"Calm down," said Cal.

"Calm down. Easy for you to say. You're not the lead on this. This is my case. And I bet that damn woman calls L.A. and then they'll know—"

"Stop it. Stop it right this minute," Cal raised her voice just a bit.

"Don't you ever curse? Don't you ever drink? What are you, the Virgin Mary? Narcotic Addicts Anonymous. Maybe I was wrong. Maybe you're the group leader. I never met anyone so prim and proper. Don't you even fart?" Denny was driving erratically in traffic. A horn blared at them; Denny ignored it.

"Pull over," said Cal.

Denny kept going.

"I said pull over."

Denny kept going.

"Pull the fuck over!" Cal yelled. Denny pulled over.

"You said the magic word," he said.

"I will not stoop to whatever level it is that you're on," Cal said. "How does it feel, when you think you're going to be in the hot seat, when you're not in control anymore? I'm sick of your attitude. Your foul mouth and your stories. What if that woman who was dragged into that car was flat chested. Would you have let her be kidnapped?"

"Makes a better story, doesn't it," Denny was actually smiling, "when she has them big tits."

"And keep the hell out of my life. You want to get me fired, score extra points with the big boys, you're going to have to fight me to the mat. I'll give you a run for your money. I'm a professional and you're not going to take that away from me."

"So Cal won't roll over and cry uncle," said Denny.

"Never have, never will."

Denny started the car up again and pulled back into traffic. "I don't know your vices, but you got more on the ball than I thought. Maybe I could put in a good word for you, you clean up your act some."

"I don't have an act," said Cal. "And I don't need a good word. I don't want a promotion someday. I want to stay doing what I'm doing, out on the street. Don't want a job telling other people what to do and how to do it."

"Don't want more money?"

"I didn't say I didn't want more money," said Cal, a smile creeping into one corner of her mouth. "Pull over . . . now!"

"Damn, woman, what now?"

"Pull over, look at this."

"I can drive and look."

"And kill us both in the bargain."

Denny pulled into a convenience store parking lot.

"Look at both of these certificates." Cal held them out so Denny could see them. "Tell me what's different."

Denny shut off the motor.

"Well, one's got that silver seal. The other one has no seal." Denny had pulled them out of Cal's hands and he peered at them. "And it's blank where the father's name should go, on both of them." Denny handed them back to Cal.

"Not only does the birth certificate not have the seal, but check out the signature. See the death certificate signature line, it's signed by the clerk in blue ink. The birth certificate's only a photocopy."

"So?" Denny's eyes narrowed.

"Why did she give us a certified copy of the death certificate and only a copy of the birth document? Why not just copies of both?"

"Like who cares?" said Denny. He appeared relieved Cal hadn't noticed something truly major that he had missed.

"That woman isn't on my list for most beloved claimants of all time," Cal said honestly.

"But she's not on the FBI's most wanted either," Denny said.

"I got a hinky feeling back there," Cal said.

Denny started the engine. "Then that's good enough for me. Where to?"

Cal looked at him with amazement. All this time, the swearing, the attitude, the reckless speeding; she had thought Denny was against her when she had been nothing more, or less, than one of the boys to him.

"Did you follow me last night?" she asked him quickly, thinking of her male attacker passed out cold in the hallway.

"Nah, I took in one of the shows."

"You didn't follow me to the Old Players Club?"

"Now, that sounds like a good time."

"Why'd you follow me the night before?"

"Like a game. Checkers, chess, checkmate. Games of skill. Game of chance."

"I thought you were out to get me," said Cal.

"Give anyone enough rope . . ." said Denny leaving the rest of the saying unspoken.

Pictures of Tony twisted in Cal's mind, his heavy link bracelet jangled as she raised her hand to her forehead.

"You got something else you want to say, say it," Denny said.

"Let's find out where they keep the records in this town," was all Cal said.

. . .

The clerk at the Department of Vital Statistics for Washoe County was a gorgeous blond in her early thirties. She and Denny would have made a perfect couple posing for wedding cake pictures. But alas, it was not to be, thought Cal, as she watched the confrontation between the two unfold.

"How far back do your records go?" Denny had asked, the two certificates from Violetta Fanny in one hand. "I'm looking into the birth and death of a kid who just died at age four."

"We have both hard copy and fiche going back that far," the clerk said, looking at whatever Denny was holding.

"I need to see your birth records for this kid." Denny put the photocopy down on the counter.

"If you have the record," said the clerk, "why do you want to see it?" She was clearly puzzled. "Also, these are not public records. Do you need a certified copy, and if so, who are you?"

"Private investigator," said Denny. "I'm working on an insurance case."

"I'm sorry, but investigators do not have access to our records," said the clerk. "Police can," she added.

Denny's eyes lit up. Swiftly he took out his wallet and flashed his ID.

"L.A.," said the clerk, clearly not impressed. "No out-of-state police. It's got to come through local law enforcement."

"Get me a phone," said Denny.

"There's a pay phone down the corridor." The clerk was holding her ground. Cal would have enjoyed this except for

163

the fact that she wanted the record as much as Denny, if not more.

Denny began to stomp out the door when the clerk called out to him. He turned, a smile starting to flourish. He thought he was getting his way.

"And we don't take authorization over the phone. The records have to be subpoenaed," called the clerk. Denny's nascent smile vanished.

Half an hour later, he and Cal stood before the counter again; it all had been cleared with a supervisor upstairs. Denny had called in all his chips with the local heat.

"Okay," said the clerk in the same tone she had used with Denny before, "what's the last name? And it's only the birth record you need to see?"

"That's right," Cal finally spoke. "What does it mean when the certificate doesn't have the solid embossed silver seal?"

"It's not a legal document," said the clerk.

"The last name is Fanny," Cal read off the photocopy, "first name Robert."

The clerk turned to the microfiche cards and then inserted the correct one into the machine. "Fanny, not a common—" She looked up at Denny and flushed. "Don't see a Robert. Let's see Bobby or Bob. Nothing. I'll check the hard copies in case there's been a problem when cataloguing the fiche." The clerk went over to some file cabinets in the corner. "Nothing here either. There's some Fannys"—again she flushed more deeply—"but no Roberts or variations. Let me see your photocopy, just to be certain you're in the right county." She walked back over to them. "That's my signature there, on that death certificate. But the birth certificate. I thought you said this boy was born four years ago?"

"Yes, he was only four when he died last month," said Cal.

"This signature. It's signed by a lady who worked here before me."

"So?" said Denny.

"I started working here ten years ago and she died of cancer a year after she retired."

18

"EVERYTHING," SAID DENNY ON the phone to Orella, "we want everything you can find on a Violetta Fanny."

"Have him run that license plate also. Nevada tag 1HOELE," said Cal, standing next to Denny near a wall lined with pay phones at the casino. Denny repeated the instruction to Orella.

"He wants to talk to you," Denny said, handing the phone unceremoniously to Cal. Cal hoped he would decide to wander off, but no such luck.

"Hey, Orella, what's up?" she said casually.

"How's our ex-friend Lazio?" asked Orella.

"I recall that case," said Cal. Her headache began, as if on cue.

"Mission successful?"

"That claimant was very difficult to locate," said Cal. "I don't think the previous skip tracer had much luck."

"Wickerstaff's right there?"

"Right on."

"You need more leads."

"I'll say."

"They're going to fry both of our asses."

"I have the utmost confidence in you," said Cal with a smile at Denny, who was glued to her every word but was pretending otherwise.

"Shit," said Orella.

"Have a good day," said Cal.

"Lord Almighty," said Denny Wickerstaff, his face drained of color, even waxen in the harsh fluorescent lighting of the coroner's office. "I've stood in on many an autopsy in my years on the force, but there's something about a child kinda knocks you akilter." He placed the pictures back down on the table.

Cal, almost against her will, picked them up. She looked at them carefully, detached, clinically. She had to.

"Strangulation," said Dr. Raab, the pathologist. She was Middle Eastern with a barely discernible accent. Her eyes were capable of sparkling but they were serious at this moment. She wore a spotless lab coat, her hair was thick and short and neatly groomed. She wore not a trace of makeup, not even lipstick.

"Asphyxia," she went on, as if prompted by the silence in the room, "due to ligature strangulation."

Cal paused at the purple face, the indentation of the string quite visible. "Dr. Raab, Mr. Wickerstaff and I are looking into this accident on behalf of the insurance carrier for the casino. We are neutral parties however, in that we are not starting out biased. We are simply trying to gather information.

"Even though this appears to be an accident, we've still come across some details that have raised questions instead of answering them."

Dr. Raab nodded. Cal put the pictures down on the table. Denny turned his head away.

"Was there anything, anything at all, that was out of the ordinary in your findings?" asked Cal.

Dr. Raab stood and both the investigators glanced up quickly at her abrupt movement. Denny looked somewhat relieved, as if he would be glad to hear that the pathologist had a negative response.

The doctor however said nothing for a long moment, linked her hands behind her back, and faced her own diploma on the wall as if she were about to retake the Hippocratic oath.

"In an autopsy," she began, turning to face them again, "it is fairly standard procedure to do full-body X-rays. Especially with children. We check for indications of child abuse," she said, and took up some notes from the Robert Fanny file. "But in this case, X-rays would not ordinarily have been done, because of the violent accidental nature of the death."

Denny took a deep breath; he still hadn't regained his color.

"But in this case, we did," said Dr. Raab, her black eyes locking with Cal's steady gaze. "The technician had noticed the child's right hand was in an abnormal position and pointed it out to me. I thought perhaps it might have been significant in that perhaps the child had grabbed the escalator railing and because of some abnormality couldn't close his hand.

"Upon palpating the hand, I found abnormalities of the fingers. We did do the X-rays," said Dr. Raab. "It had raised a flag, however small in my mind. You have to realize that open fractures would be impossible to distinguish from injuries possibly sustained in the accident.

"But another thing—external examination showed the hand to be swollen but not discolored."

"And what were your findings after x-raying him?" Denny couldn't wait.

"We found partially healed fractures, every finger. Callus formation indicated joints had been dislocated or injured in the past."

"My God," said Cal, covering her eyes.

"Severely dislocated or injured," said Dr. Raab.

"What makes you think there could have been a problem here, Doc?" asked Denny.

"It appeared the child had never received medical attention for those fractures. They would have been splinted and healed or healing."

"I gotta get some air," said Denny, and jumped for the door.

"With an accident like this, I suppose the parents will be looking for a settlement," said Dr. Raab privately to Cal now that Denny had left.

"We will look into this very closely, Dr. Raab, of this we can assure you," said Cal.

"Private investigator," said the doctor, looking at Cal's card, "maybe some good will come out of this which has been bothering me."

"I don't imagine many things bother you after all these years doing autopsies," said Cal.

"No, not very often," said the doctor, "but this one, this one did." The doctor shook her head sadly. "I'll see you to the door."

"I can find my own way," said Cal.

"I think you can," said the doctor. "I know you can."

"You have a difficult job, Doctor."

"I uncover the secrets that the body may hold," said Dr. Raab. "But you must uncover the evil that lurks in people's souls. Your job is by far the more difficult, Miss Brantley."

19

"HIGH DESERT'S WHAT THEY call this," said Denny. He had a jaunty elbow out the window of the late model brown rental car.

"I don't like it, I don't like any of it," said Cal.

"What is it? Spell it out. I'm all ears, seeing that we got numerous miles to go before we sleep," said Denny. He fiddled with the radio dial and got only static.

"I don't want to be negative so I'll just say that it was a good idea leaving the Firebird back at the casino. Way you drive we'd run that car right into the ground."

"And the ground is where you'd end up out here with car trouble," said Denny. "See that soft sand shoulder on the side of the road—get stuck there, it's all over."

"You're always so cheerful," said Cal.

"Reality, lady. Better learn to deal with it. Know you're only part of the big food chain."

"Spare me," said Cal, holding up a hand. "What time did you tell Mr. Comstock we'd be in Rachel?"

"Our witness with the Bowie knife. Royce, Roy, as he asked me to call him, said anytime was fine between sunup and sundown. Said he's been sticking close to home since he got bit by a scorpion."

"I love this place. I simply love this state," said Cal. She looked out at the expanse of road before them, going straight ahead in a long ribbon.

Mountains were strung along on both sides in the distance and glistening white patches of alkali flats stretched across the desert. Except for plant life, which mainly consisted of cactus, mesquite, yucca, and the gray-green sagebrush, there hadn't been much of anything else. Cal remarked that there wasn't much of anything alive.

"Nothing much living out here," said Denny in response to her remark. "Lady, you don't know the half of it. I been through here once before, comin' up from Vegas. I don't know what possessed me to drive instead of flying. Needed some time to think, I guess it was. Well, a Nevada state trooper told me going east from Tonopah you're going the closest to nowhere you can get. Take a side dirt road for miles. Dump a body. There are these old mine shafts go down for hundreds of feet into the ground. Ideal dumping areas. In fact there are stories—"

"Spare me. Please," Cal cut him off, looking into his flat cold gray eyes.

"And you've heard about Area 51?"

"No, what's that?" asked Cal. She rubbed her neck but it was her back that really hurt today. She wanted to ask Denny to stop but she didn't want to get out of the car here; she wanted the car to just keep going and going.

"There's talk of UFOs being spotted out here."

"Well, I can see that, aliens liking this. If they wanted a really desolate place, this is it. So we've got scorpions, old mine shafts for dumping bodies, and now UFOs."

"You're a good listener," Denny said easily. He was not getting as riled by her today. Maybe it was getting on the open road. Speeding along at eighty-five miles an hour siphoned off some of his nervous energy.

"There's also a top-secret military base where they're supposed to have bodies of some of the aliens."

"Now, that's neat," said Cal.

"And we're heading right towards it," said Denny.

"Adventureland, here we come," said Cal. "All this and we're getting paid for it."

"What do you make of the case so far?" said Denny about seventy miles later. Cal had gotten into the rhythm of not talking and she didn't answer right away. She watched him try the radio knob again. Denny attempting to listen to music; Denny wanting to talk. A spiritual transformation in the middle of a place that didn't even have a bathroom.

"You know I've got to admit that you uncovering those things, the phony birth certificate, the kid's broken fingers. That was good. You're good, lady. I have to hand you that."

"Thanks, but no thanks." Cal's voice was a croak. "I don't need to prove myself to you, or anyone."

"Hey, don't jump on my case."

"Don't forget the label," said Cal.

"Label? What label?"

"The jacket, remember?"

Denny shook his head. "You think that's tied into this too?"

"I don't know what to think yet. I hope Orella will come through with some more leads." She was glad she no longer had to hide contacts with Orella now that he was doing some digging on their current case as well as the Tony trail.

"Leads to what?"

"Don't know yet. Maybe nothing. Maybe we'll figure out something that will help our client."

"Is that all you care about," said Denny, "the client?"

"We've been over this ground before, Denny. The kid's dead, that's a proven. Let it rest. Does this rental car have a tape player? I brought along a Santana tape. I think better to music." To Cal's amazement, he said, "Go ahead, put it on." Cal put the tape on.

"Dead kid. I can't let it be," he said after a while.

"You saw the pictures. It's done."

"Man, if only—" Denny shook his head.

"Did you know Mark Fuhrman?" Cal asked in an attempt to change the subject.

" 'Course I knew Fuhrman."

"Did O. J. really do it?"

"Does a bear jack off in the woods?"

"Were you involved in that murder investigation?" asked Cal.

"Nah, I was outta there by then. But did I ever tell you about the time I was off duty and these two punks came into the bank where I was making a deposit? . . ."

20

"**LIFE IS GOOD,**" **SAID** Denny, munching on a Mc-
Donald's creation that had just dripped ketchup onto his
Hawaiian print shirt. "Hey, is that all you're going to eat?"

"Tonopah," she said dreamily, "Tonopah," and she took
another bite out of her Power bar. There had been buildings
and bathrooms and juice drinks. Nearly heaven. Cal thought
about how the desert raised your level of appreciation of the
basics.

Now the desert stretched out before them again. She was
a city girl through and through. Lizards and diamondback
rattlers and packrats and tarantulas, this was their land, not
hers. She regarded a Joshua tree as if it were an alien on the
march. The Golden Gate rose up in her thoughts and a traffic
jam might even be a welcome experience after this. Her
pager went off.

"Probably Orella," she said to Denny, scrambling to see
the number. "Yup."

She tried her cell phone. "Can't get a dial tone," she said crossly, "out of range. Damn."

"We'll have to wait till Rachel," said Denny. "They'll have regular phones there."

"You sure you took the right road out of Tonopah?" asked Cal nervously.

"I got an inner compass. We're heading in the right direction. What, worried we're going into the east? Those old mine shafts?" Denny gave a short laugh.

"I want to get there already," said Cal with more than a trace of rancor. If she had to be stranded in the desert she didn't want it to be with Denny Wickerstaff.

"Sign coming up," Denny said, actually slowing down.

"That's a good one," said Cal. "Extraterrestrial Highway. Someone has a good sense of humor."

"Have to, out here," said Denny. "There's my kind of sign," he said as they passed another one. "Speed limit warp 7." He stepped on the gas.

"It's all probably just a bunch of hype," said Cal thoughtfully. "All this alien nonsense. They've gone pretty far to get tourists out here. Otherwise it would be just nothing."

"Still looks like nothing to me," said Denny.

"I never thought we'd see the day we'd agree on something," said Cal. "And if there ever is a next time that we have to come out here, bring a real compass."

"My dick is my compass," said Denny.

"Rachel, Nevada," said Cal. "A town where the elevation is more than the population."

"Got that address for Royce Comstock? I want to get in and then get the hell out," said Denny.

"No way," said Cal. "I can't drive another mile today."

"We're going to stay overnight? I wonder if there are any good cathouses in the vicinity. Feel like I could get lucky."

"Get lucky when you have to pay for it?" said Cal.

"All a woman has to do is walk into a bar near closing. I don't care if she's sixty years old, she'll get laid. What about you, Cal? Think you'll get lucky in Rachel? And"—Denny was slowing to park the car—"don't get all hot and bothered about sexual harassment. I don't mean getting lucky with me. Furthest thing from my mind."

"Furthest thing from mine too, Denny. Well, we're here. And funny thing, Mr. Wickerstaff, I do feel kind of lucky. Wonder what kind of men hang around a place like this?"

"I'm real glad you said that word, Cal. The word men. Tell you the truth, I was beginning to wonder about you."

"I'm not going to respond to that. Contrary to what you might think, I don't always have to get the last word in."

"What about Orella? Don't you think you should call him? See what the latest skivvy is."

"You want to get started with the witness?"

"Witless or witness? It's okay. I'm in no rush, I'll wait for you. You seem to have a way with people."

"Why, Denny. That's one of the few nice things you've said. . . ."

"Don't get a swelled head. I just meant people seem comfortable lying to you."

21

"**WICKERSTAFF'S WAITING IN THE** car," Cal told Orella from a pay phone. "He's been nice to me all day, definitely not himself."

"Watch your back," warned Orella, "something could be up."

"I sat in the Old Players Club last night again till midnight," said Cal.

"Anything?"

"I won fourteen dollars. You gotta know when to fold."

"I figure we can get into the credit card stuff maybe one more time. I'm almost all out of pretexts."

"Let's wait on it then till I'm out of here. We won't leave until morning. I couldn't do anything about a lead now if I wanted to. How about our lady?"

"Miss Fanny? Yeah, I got some stuff. But I tell ya, if you're digging deep on this one, there'll be no gusher." Cal didn't interrupt Orella when he got talking like this; he was just getting wound up.

"So spill," she said briefly.

"Forty-eight years old, born in Virginia City, Nevada. No marriage or divorce records in the state. Parents deceased. No credit applied for, ever. No hits on local bank accounts."

"What do you make of that?"

"She pays cash. Then banks offshore or out of the country."

"Go on," said Cal, intrigued.

"No records of any wages through social security. Keep that out of any reports, now, that's a mean one to tangle with. Never filed tax returns."

"Never?" Cal's voice was even. "How is she getting her money? Inheritance?"

"Far as I could see the old people died about eight years apart. Left her some property, with a house in Virginia City. The house in Sparks is a rental; she's not the owner."

"Give me more," said Cal. "How about kids. Any children?"

"Keeping your inquiries low-key since this Virginia City is probably tight-knit, we gagged one source who knew of one child. Didn't recall if it was a boy or girl or even a name." Cal didn't like using gag or pretext calls, but they were routinely used to obtain information.

"How about court cases?"

"We checked Storey County, but they're not on-line yet. We called a local contact and they did an in-person record check. She's clean in Storey except for one case, which is in storage. They've ordered it and it'll be ready in two days."

Orella read the number off to Cal and she made a quick note of it.

"Washoe County, she's clean. Again, we needed an in-person, but these I can bill to the file. She's always gone by the name of Violetta, far as anything that we've turned up. We checked Nevada worker comp records, they're on the database and go back ten years. No hit."

"Hmmm," said Cal.

"Oh, yeah, one more thing. In Nevada the casinos can serve as banks. It's nearly impossible to crack those, but we gagged most of the major ones, took a bit of finessing, but it appeared there were no accounts. Same goes for the federal credit unions. They absolutely will not give up anything; it's easier to get a direct line into the White House." Orella paused; he needed praise.

"Good job," said Cal. "I doubt she'd go with federal since she hasn't filed tax returns, unless we're talking about a minimal amount of interest."

"Good point," said Orella. Cal needed stroking now and then also. "Now, about that license plate—"

"Yeah, the plate," said Cal, casting a glance at Denny through the front windshield. He was just sitting there peacefully; decidedly not himself.

"Comes back to—get this name—a Tuesday Hoele."

"That's a good one," remarked Cal.

"But wait, check this out. We popped the address, someplace in Hawthorne and the phone number is listed for Miss Kitty's Palomino Ranch. A brothel." Orella was losing it now; people in L.A. always got a big charge out of this type of information. Cal let him have his fun. For a minute.

"Okay, give me the address." Cal thought of the Filipino woman in back of the child on the escalator. "This could be an important witness."

"I can handle this part of the investigation for you, Cal. It'll get me some more field experience."

"You'll probably have to fight Wickerstaff for the honors. Any background on Miss Tuesday?"

"Filipino registered alien. Twenty-eight years old. Nothing in the courts. No credit. Almost doesn't exist as far as a paper trail. These are tough ones," said Orella.

"Filipino!" Cal exclaimed. "Maybe we're going to hit pay dirt." She saw Denny motioning. "I need to go now, we're interviewing a witness. Let me know when you run that final stuff for me, okay?" Cal didn't want to say too much on the phone; it made her paranoid.

Orella said good-bye and hung up, his voice had been a comfort even over the long-distance phone lines. Cal hung up the receiver. Tony's ID bracelet felt like a ball and chain on her wrist. Her head and back throbbed. This case could make her old. She turned and exited the phone booth and smiled at Wickerstaff, which was the last thing she felt like doing. Denny smiled back.

Royce Comstock's old ramshackle cabin had not seen paint in years. A strong breeze had kicked up and stirred the glass-and-metal wind chimes clanging from a corrugated roof.

The sound belonged more to the spirit world than reality, and Cal shivered as she looked around at the barren landscape. Who would choose to live out here? Well, she was about to find out.

Two magpies landed in a patch of nearby dirt and pecked at something in the cheat grass. Others nimbly hopped around an old car hulk and some rusting mining parts.

"Teach 'em to talk like a parrot," said a man, opening the front door before they had time to knock. The wind chimes gave an answering sound in the silence. Cal, who was not often tongue-tied, waited for Denny to speak first.

"Roy Comstock," he said, offering his hand to Denny, then to Cal.

"Mostly scavengers out here, huh?" said Denny. Cal decided Denny's newfound shyness was a result of his being totally out of his element, as she felt herself.

"We're all scavengers out'n these parts. Crows, hawks, maybe an eagle once in a while," he continued. "And then again there's those sail rabbits."

"Sail rabbits?" asked Denny. "Never heard of those." His words were punctuated by the wind chimes kicking up again. "Did you want us to interview you out here, or"—here Denny paused for a split second—"inside?"

"Rabbit carcasses," said Comstock, his blue eyes flashing behind granny glasses. "That's sail rabbits. Cars run over them jackrabbits out there on the highway. They dry out and are as flat as paper and you kin peel 'em off the road and sail 'em across the desert." Comstock chuckled. Cal realized they were the ideal captive audience; Comstock hadn't had any visitors in a while and he must have lots of what he supposed was neat stuff to share.

"What kind of people live out here in the high desert country?" Cal asked.

"The Question Lady," Comstock said, and tugged at his neat gray ponytail. A diamond stud in his earlobe flashed. "Well, what you mean is, who is crazy enough to want to be out here? Loners, pure and simple, yes, that's who. Loners." Comstock began to look thoughtful. "Old grizzled miners. Prospectors. Hippies, because there is no such thing as an ex-hippie. Burned-out druggies and UFO believers." Cal found herself staring at his snakeskin boots. Didn't see those much in San Francisco. "And then there's yer nut cases, pure and simple. Yessir. And I bet ya'll wonderin' exactly what category I fall into? Maybe you'd even like to make sure of it before you step inside."

"Hopefully not the last category," Cal joked. Denny looked like he was mentally tallying his available fire power. Afterward he'd probably lecture Cal on why situations like these were a lesson in never letting your guard down.

"I'm a writer," said Comstock, "and depending on your point of view, could very well fit into several of those pigeonholes. Anticipating your next inquiry, my genre . . . I consider myself heir to the Castaneda legacy."

"Carlos Castaneda?" asked Cal.

"Yes. Are you familiar with this author's works?" Comstock looked straight at Cal now.

"My mom went to Berkeley," Cal said, as if that answered

the question. "I used to sneak peeks at her library."

"*The Teachings of Don Juan* must have been spirited reading for a young girl," said Comstock.

"Well, possibly the deeper meanings of learning to fly and growing a beak went over my head," admitted Cal.

"You've lost me," Denny said.

"You're like those magpies over there," said Comstock, "having not yet reached the plateau of higher consciousness."

"My conscience is just fine, thank you," responded Denny, a hint of his old self returning abruptly.

"Castaneda wrote about his trip through the desert with a sorcerer, an old Yaqui Indian that he had met in a Greyhound bus station." Cal threw that in, knowing Denny would relish that fact.

"Then," Comstock took up the thread, "under Don Juan's tutelage, he experimented with peyote, jimson weed, and mushrooms in an effort to achieve another way of reality."

"Everything I hated about the sixties. And the seventies," Denny growled.

"I suppose you're a Vietnam veteran," said Comstock.

"Never served," said Denny. "Bad feet."

An old woman, dressed in a long, flowing skirt and a black leather vest, her bare arms covered with long, curling dragon tattoos, appeared suddenly from around the side of the house. She stared at them with unfriendly dark eyes.

"My woman," said Comstock simply. "She is Shoshone. A medicine woman."

The breeze whipped Cal's hair across her face and the wind chimes clanged madly. She stole a glance at the leathery-skinned woman, not wanting to have their eyes meet.

"Let's go inside, we can talk more there. And perhaps you'll like something to drink or eat." Comstock's eyes were as serene as a summer sky as he opened the door.

The inside of the cabin was small, dark, and dirty. An old portable typewriter was perched on the dining table. Comstock moved it aside so they had unimpaired views of each other.

"I prefer to write drafts in longhand," he explained, "but publishers won't look at them. Therefore the concession to modern times."

There were crumbs of food on the table and a small globule of what could have been dried ketchup. Cal checked the seat of her chair before she sat down, but she did so surreptitiously. Comstock's sharp eyes missed nothing. Neither did Cal's. "Writers use computers now," she pointed out with a smile.

Comstock pondered that for a short moment before he responded. "And so they do," he said, "but the typewriter will suffice. It's bad enough being pushed into the twentieth century, let alone the twenty-first. I refuse to even allow electricity to flow through our abode, be it ever so humble."

"You don't even use a generator for small appliances?" asked Denny.

Comstock shook his head. "Broke down two years ago. Never got it repaired."

"May we tape?" Cal brought out the micro-cassette recorder.

"Well, at least you asked," replied Comstock, eyeing the small piece of equipment with distrust. There was the lingering odor of something that had been burnt, the smell of acrid ashes. Denny was looking around with interest, as if there were the possibility of a drug bust.

"Roy, you any relation to the Comstock's of the Virginia City area? Don't they call that place the Queen of the Comstock?" asked Denny. Cal looked at her partner with some amazement.

"Henry Comstock, a con man and conniver. Co-owner of every mine in sight. From what I heard tell my forefather lived only for today and for the good things in life he earned with his prospecting efforts." Comstock had taken out a penknife and was fiddling with it.

"What's wrong with that?" asked Denny, keeping an eye on the knife.

"Material things are only of the material world," said Comstock. "They don't bring eternal happiness, or real power. Why, that entire area came to be known as the Comstock Lode, for all the good it did Henry. Sold out for a mere eleven thousand dollars and ended his life with a revolver. The others didn't fare much better, died in paupers' graves or insane asylums." Comstock shook his head.

Comstock's woman sat away from them in a corner chair.

The inside of the cabin was cold and she had started a fire in the hearth. The flames shot up as the fire took, and black shadows played and leaped against the wall. The whites of the medicine woman's eyes seemed red with the fire's glow.

Cal began the tape player and got Comstock going with his rendition of the events at the casino. Comstock broke off briefly to speak to the woman in her native tongue, apparently asking her to serve both Cal and Denny with tea. Cal didn't touch it, but noticed Denny took a few absentminded sips. The brew was black and had a peppermint smell.

"How is your tea, miss?" Comstock inquired.

"Thank you for offering it, but during the day I only drink water," said Cal firmly.

"Can I offer you some water?" said Comstock.

"No, thanks, I've already got some with me," responded Cal. "Now, Mr. Comstock—Roy," Cal continued, "may I ask why you were in the casino that day?"

"Several times a year we go into Reno," said Comstock directly. "Diversion, supplies."

"Did you drink any alcohol that day, in the preceding twenty-four hours?"

"No."

"Had you taken any prescription drugs that day?"

"No."

"How about any nonprescription drugs?" asked Denny bluntly.

Comstock thought for a moment. "Did some mushrooms as I recall the night before."

"Aren't those powerful hallucinogens?" Denny asked.

"Reaching higher consciousness can be a hard-won wisdom," said Comstock. "There are not only moments of ecstasy but of stark panic." He rolled up his pants leg to show them an ugly-looking wound. "Couple of days ago, we went into the desert at night, did some peyote buttons. Bad, bad trip. Nothing but scorpions out there, crawling everywhere, hundreds, maybe thousands of them."

"Real scorpions?" asked Cal, aware that the tape was still rolling.

"As Castaneda would term it, perhaps a separate reality," answered Comstock. "But real enough. Too real," Comstock looked over at the Indian woman. "Punishment perhaps for my indulgence in earthly pleasures. I've been known to spend some time at the Palomino Ranch." His gaze swung back to meet Cal's unblinking eyes.

"Were you tripping at the time of the incident in the casino, Roy?" This from Denny.

"Tripping? Why, no. The effects of the mushrooms had quite worn off."

"Had you eaten anything that day?" asked Cal.

"You mean mushrooms?" asked Comstock, apparently confused by the question.

"No, just regular food." Cal said.

Comstock thought, and then responded, "Yes, I recall we had eaten a meal."

"Where?" said Denny in a clipped tone.

"A breakfast place near the El Dorado," said Comstock.

"Tell us what happened in your own words," Cal said in

a softer tone, trying to get Denny off track and keep Comstock from stalling out.

"You mean after breakfast?" The witness was getting flustered. Denny's tone was too abrupt.

"With the boy, with the boy," growled Denny.

"Just take your time, Mr. Comstock, we realize it must have been a very upsetting experience," Cal put in soothingly.

"I saw the boy coming down the escalator," the man began to recall, looking down at the table.

"What first drew your attention to him?" asked Cal in a low voice.

"My woman—my woman had grabbed my arm and pointed at him." Comstock stopped and didn't go on. Denny frowned and started to open his mouth.

"Denny," Cal said, and when he looked at her, she shook her head with a warning look. "Your woman had pointed," Cal urged him calmly, "then what happened? Why did she point?"

"She saw—saw the boy's aura."

"Let me speak, Roy." The woman stood up and advanced toward the table. She was about sixty, but her skin had taken the weathering of the elements and was charred brown with deep facial creases. Her arms were scored by wrinkling folds and they undulated, making the dragon tattoos appear as if they were writhing.

For the first time Cal's eyes met with the woman's stony black ones. A faint smile seemed to lurk in the recesses of the crone's wrinkled mouth.

The Shoshone woman held up her hand. Comstock fell silent and even Denny appeared transfixed. "I had seen the boy in a vision. Even before what happened that day, I had known he was in great danger, that he was suffering. His fall, his death relieved him of his suffering."

"I don't get this," said Denny, throwing his pen down on the table. "You knew this was going to happen?"

The Shoshone woman nodded.

"Then why didn't you stop it?"

"I cannot interfere. But Roy, he tried. He tried to help."

"So," Cal interrupted, "you had a dream about this child, this boy. Did you know him? Had you ever seen him before?"

"Only in the vision," said the woman.

"Do you know any more about this suffering you say you saw?" Cal asked.

"No. Only that he had lost the protection of his guardian spirit."

Denny shook his head. The Indian woman's eyes flashed angrily.

"You do not believe?" she said to Denny, who didn't respond. "And you, you do not believe?" she asked of Cal.

The acrid odor inside the cabin had increased and it was growing smoky and warm. The woman's words seem to echo inside Cal's mind. Comstock's eyes had lost their placid look and were now sharp and piercing, his mouth set in a tight, unforgiving line.

"I'm still looking for the answers and not knowing the questions," said Cal slowly.

"I tried—I tried to get to him," said Comstock. "It was his time. But I tried."

"Tell me more," said Cal, "tell me about the boy's mother."

"I didn't see no mother around," said Roy.

"The blond woman, the large blond woman," prompted Denny. "You didn't see her?"

"I didn't have time to see any blondes," Roy answered.

"I see the woman with the third eye," said the medicine woman looking at Cal. "I see evil all around." Her eyes closed and she was swaying.

Denny threw the pen back down on the table with disgust.

"Anything else that you recall, Mr. Comstock, anything else we haven't covered?"

"It was his time," said Comstock, "and, as my woman says, it was for the best."

"But you had never seen the boy before, Roy? You didn't know him?" asked Cal.

"Had I seen him before? No, never," said Comstock emphatically.

"And you didn't know the large blond woman standing in front of him?"

"No."

"And there's another woman. The one standing in back of the boy," said Denny, "possibly a Filipino woman. Did you know her?"

"Nope," said Comstock.

"Have you understood all our questions?" said Cal.

"Yes."

"And all your answers were true and correct to the best of your knowledge and belief?"

"Yes."

"And you were aware that I was recording?"

"Yes."

"Thank you, then. The statement is concluded."

"I never heard such a crock in my life," said Denny. They were back outside at the car. Cal looked at the cabin, smoke now curling from a vent in the tin roof. "Scorpions, mushrooms, visions. Talk about unreliable witnesses. And that hag, she was one wrinkled-up old bag," said Denny unkindly.

"That typewriter," said Cal thoughtfully, "it was an electric model."

"So?"

"He did say that they had no electricity. It's been a while since he sent anything to a publisher."

"Probably too high," said Denny.

"No, wait," Cal said, "stop and think about this for a minute. This guy Comstock comes out of the crowd. He was the one ready to take action. He's the one who doesn't just stand there."

"That's what happens when you're blasted out of your skull. You're loose as a goose. Medicine men in Greyhound bus stations. Give me a break."

"But he was ready," Cal said one more time, mostly to herself, her mind whirling with possibilities, her memory branded with the Indian woman's red stare. "And he's lied. Wonder just how much."

22

"**TOURISTS USUALLY LIKE THE** Little A'Le'Inn." The lady with the waist-long gray braided hair was polite but not overly friendly. "Hard Copy was there filming last year. Other news shows, magazines, been out." She began to ring up Cal's purchases at the convenience store.

"I never had much use for TV," Cal replied, "and I'd just as soon stay out of the news. Any other places?"

The woman made a strange sound, something between a chuckle and a hawking noise. "What you see is what you get in Rachel. Ain't no undiscovered party places. There is one watering hole aside from the Little A'Le'Inn that the locals hang out at. It's called the End of the Line. There's no sign up. No need to advertise, everyone knows where the place is. There's a green light flashin', you can't miss it." The woman's mouth suddenly tightened, as if she decided she had said enough. "That'll be thirty-two fifty."

Cal wanted to get the woman talking more, but instinct told her that, for whatever reason, she was shutting down.

"You know," she said casually, "I saw that sign down the street—spaceship and alien crossing—are there really aliens around here?"

"Only ones I've seen are the tourists who come to this town," the woman replied. Then she gave Cal her change and some precise directions to the End of the Line.

They ate at a greasy spoon and then checked into a motel that made the Lucky Motel look like the Taj Mahal. Cal told Denny about the End of the Line and he said he'd join her in a while. He wanted to leave early in the morning and get out of town. Their mission was accomplished. Place gave him the creeps, he added in an uncharacteristic remark. Cal noted that he didn't look well. He had picked at his dinner (which was understandable given the food) but had only finished half of his beer. Once or twice he had shivered as if he were coming down with something, and his skin had an unhealthy pallor.

"We'll leave early." He shut the door to his room, which was next to hers.

Cal didn't bother to unpack or change out of her jeans. She took one look at the four walls of her room and headed out on the town.

The woman at the convenience store had lied. The End of the Line did have a sign. It was handprinted and partly falling off the front of the building. The green strobe light that the woman had mentioned was there as promised, maybe it guided alien ships into a landing pattern.

It was a jukebox joint, dark, smoky, and crowded. Hearing the blaring music lifted Cal's spirits immediately. People looked around at her, and when they saw her, conversations actually ceased. The ensuing silence made Cal feel as if she had stepped into a B movie. Stranger in town enters a local watering hole, is eyed with suspicion and caution as she steps up to the bar and asks for a drink.

"What'll it be, miss?" said the bartender as if he hoped she'd just ask for directions and blast on out of there.

White wine wasn't in the movie script so Cal got a Coors Lite. Then she turned casually to face the staring hordes. The last time she had gotten so much attention in a crowd she had trailed toilet paper out from the john along on her shoe.

She smiled, thinking how absolutely wonderful it was going to be to get the hell out of this place in the morning. She hoped Denny didn't have a fever or the flu and that they would be laid up here until he was well enough to make the return trip.

An old Van Halen tune came on the jukebox and Cal looked to see who was putting quarters in the old-fashioned machine. A man with long blond hair down to his shoulders turned from it and stared in her direction.

Actually she couldn't tell where he was looking since he had on mirrored aviator glasses. But he was cruising in her direction. Then he was right in front of her, talking to her.

"Harley," the man said, and offered forth a cool hand. Cal noted a turquoise ring and a moderately expensive watch.

"I didn't know aliens rode Harleys," Cal responded, winning an immediate laugh.

"My name is Harley," he said, "and I hope we won't get off to a bad start."

"I'm Cal, and no, in a place like this, how in the world could anything be bad?"

"I've been here a week," Harley said, "and I've never seen you around."

"I've been here three hours and I'm frankly counting the seconds."

"Why are you here?" he asked, taking a swig of his beer.

"Just passing through," Cal said. "Why are you here a whole week? Car break down?"

Harley laughed again as if he were breaking out of a long dry spell. "Thankfully my wheels are still operable. Actually I'm heading out tomorrow, in the morning. Got enough of what I came for—enough I guess for a special interest story."

"You're a reporter?" asked Cal.

"Freelance. Never did see any aliens or spaceships, but I got enough to sell a decent piece. Interest's running high in this Area 51 right now. The New Age crowd can't get enough of it."

"I bet," said Cal.

"So, how about you? Got a boyfriend, or you drive out here all by your lone self?"

"Work," said Cal. "I'm on a business trip, and someone from my office is with me. I don't think I'd like to be out on that desert highway by myself."

"Yeah, I know what you mean," Harley agreed. "You ready for another?" he held up his beer.

"Not yet," replied Cal, eyeing the crowd. They had already lost interest in a bar pickup between outsiders.

"So, what kind of business are you in?" Harley asked.

Cal hesitated; she never felt comfortable telling people what she did. "Insurance," she said after too long a pause.

"Ah, you sell insurance?"

Cal nodded. She wondered if Denny was going to be blustering in at any second and catch her. He'd never let her live it down. Cal, caught, with some not-so-local boy.

The worst part was that thought had slithered rather quickly into Cal's overt thoughts, let alone her subconscious, which had cranked into the more wilder fantasies.

Harley took off his shades. His eyes were a vibrant green and he stepped closer to Cal. "You know, you're the first person in a long time hasn't laughed or remarked on my name."

"Yes, I did."

"Oh, that first remark. I didn't mean that. Usually everyone wants to know why my folks named me that."

"I figured we're both about the same age. Maybe you're a bit older than me," said Cal. "And your folks were major hippies."

"Hey, that's good. You're good, Cal. You'd probably make a good detective."

"I'll remember that, Harley. Thank you."

One beer later.

"Is that a girlfriend along on your business trip?" Harley asked in an innocent tone.

"Why? What do you mean?"

"I was thinking we could go get her from her room, or wherever. Maybe she'd get into a little menage à trois."

"Harley, you're stuck in the sixties, along with your name. Get real."

"Sorry. Never hurts to ask."

"Yes, it does," said Cal.

"I don't want your estimation of me to drop."

"Then watch it," said Cal. "That kind of talk turns me off."

"What kind turns you on?"

Two hours later, they were still at the bar. It was after midnight and Denny still had not showed, at least not overtly. Cal had stopped looking for him to come through the door. Or caring if he did.

"So, I was standing right below the fire escape in this hostage negotiation situation when I noticed they had sent in the entire L.A. SWAT team—" Harley was saying.

Cal was nodding with amusement when a man abruptly jostled her as he made an effort to get up to the bar.

"Well, I've seen them, Sam," he said loudly to the bartender.

"What'll it be tonight, old-timer?" asked the bartender without any great interest.

"Gin and tonic, make it a double," said the man.

Cal had moved closer to Harley as it was evident the individual hadn't bathed in quite a while. The front of his pants from waist to ankle was covered with dirt. Cal couldn't believe that someone could go out in public that filthy.

"I seen them landin' out by the Castleton's ranch. Three ships, two little ones and a mother ship. Damn mother ship was enormous. I tell you. Motherfuckin' enormous." Spittle was flying from the man's chapped lips.

"Hey, man, there are ladies present," said Harley quietly.

"Sorry, sorry," said the man. "All I ever seen in here were whores. Ain't seen a lady in so long I wouldn't know it if one blew me."

"Hey, dude, you're going to have to step outside in a minute," said Harley, not backing down.

Denny would have shot the man by now, Cal thought. "Just forget it, Harley," she said, putting a hand on his arm.

"Besides," said the man, getting back in their faces again, "I ain't responsible for my actions. They make me say the things I do."

"Who makes you say things?" asked Harley, giving Cal a sidelong look.

"Why, the aliens. The little purple guys. I been beamed up to the mother ship eight times now. I gotta tell you this. . . ." The man leaned in toward them, his breath throwing off an unpleasant stench. "They done things to me," he confided.

"What kind of things?" asked Harley. He seemed genuinely curious. *Reporters!* Cal thought.

The man downed his drink. "Buy me another? And I'll tell you a story make you pull down your pants."

"Sure, dude. You look like you could use another." Harley signaled to the bartender. "So, what's your story," Harley asked.

"Some night, a night like tonight, wind's blowin', maybe a desert storm comin' in, they beam you on up, see. Wind's kickin up so's the drug planes comin' in from Mexico off-loading their grass ain't takin' the chance. Not a sound. Then a great big light and then two smaller ones. Ships give off a hum, sort of like makes you sick to your stomach, that hum.

"And you know, that's why they got that United States of America military base here. The aliens crashed once and they got their ship and the bodies of the aliens. U.S. can't figure that equipment out in the ship, though.

"They got me up in that ship and done things. And no-body down here gives a flying—"

Harley stopped him by gripping his shoulder. The man stopped talking and started to cry, his long racking sobs filling the bar with their sound. People, however, were not paying any attention as if he had pulled this routine before.

"They planted an antenna here." The man leaned forward, showing both Harley and Cal the back of his neck. "They've got a giant eye in the sky," the man wheezed.

"They got me under their control. They're taking over. You'll see!" The man stopped and looked at Harley's eyes.

"Wait. Hold on! You're one of them, aren't you! You're in human form, you've stolen someone's body."

"No, man, calm down," said Harley. "I'm as human as you or anyone in here. I'm from L.A.," added Harley, as if that fact certified his lineage. Cal thought it nearly negated it.

The man's face was turning red, then a deep purple. He looked at Cal. "And I seen you too. You were on the mother ship. You touched me, you did things to me!" He was yelling now.

"You wish," said Cal calmly.

"Aliens! Aliens! Sound the alert! We're being invaded!"

"Okay, Mac, you're out of here," said the bartender, and he gave a nod to two men who had been standing at the bar. They each took one of the man's arms. He was screaming, and made gagging noises as they began to drag him out.

"Eye in the sky, they're watching," he yelled, and then, all at once, he was unpleasantly and violently sick. The deluge of vomit sprayed around the people nearest him, some of it landing on Cal's pants legs.

"Ugh," she said, moving back in disgust.

"Aliens," said the man as he was dragged out. "Aliens," he pointed a dirty finger straight at Cal and Harley.

23

"LONELY OUT HERE, ISN'T it?" said Harley.

"Loneliest place I've ever been," agreed Cal a little too quickly. They were in Harley's jeep. He had driven Cal back to her motel room to change out of her soiled clothes. "Well, looks like that other bar is closed. I don't know why, but I feel too wired to call it a night," Cal said.

"Adrenalin's still pumping after that character in the bar flipped out," remarked Harley. "I'm feeling it too."

"What a crazy! He actually had me looking at his neck to see if there was an antenna there."

"The worst part is that his account does match other cases found in available literature."

"But that's just the point, Harley, available literature. He can read it like everyone else."

"Yeah, I see what you're saying. Makes a great ending for my article, though. Maybe now I've even got enough for a book."

They were just driving now, heading out of town. "Is that

all experiences mean to you—material?" said Cal.

Harley didn't answer immediately. "Material, yeah, it's become material. Stinks, doesn't it, making yourself, after all is said and done, just another commodity?"

"Selling out," said Cal quietly.

"Then, afterwards, all you've got is your money to keep you company, and the best of everything it can buy."

"Can't buy people," said Cal.

"No, you can't buy love, Cal. People you can buy."

The breeze had turned into a wind. Dust and white powder off the alkali flats were blowing across the road.

"Ready to turn back?" he asked Cal.

She nodded. "Yeah, I feel better now. Getting tired."

"Don't get too tired," Harley said, "I thought we'd do some peyote buttons I picked up back at the last town."

"Man, Harley, you are stuck in a time warp. Just the thought of my mother doing drugs has been enough to make me turned off. Mom was a hippie, big-time," said Cal.

"Hey, it's cool. Look at the materialistic kids they've turned out. We don't have to revolt against everything they did."

"Harley, this isn't the time or the place to get into a debate about our parents—wait a minute!" Cal was looking upward at a point off to the right of them. "Look, look over there!"

Harley slowed the jeep. "I don't see anything." He peered through Cal's side of the vehicle.

"I thought I saw something—a light," said Cal.

Harley stopped in the middle of the road. "Yeah, maybe

I do see something over there. It's low. Real low. Now it's gone. Damn. I wish I had my camera."

"Can't you just do something without committing it to either print or film?" asked Cal.

"Yeah, one thing," said Harley, moving over and kissing her. "Ummm, I like this red dress."

"There's that light again. I've never seen anything like that. Eye in the sky, the man said," murmured Cal.

"He's spent too much time in these parts," said Harley. "He was crazy. There's no such thing as alien space—ohmygod."

"Harley. It's coming straight at us!"

The light grew brighter until it was a searing dazzling sphere that made them shield their eyes. Cal had hold of Harley's shoulder and he gripped her hand there with his.

"It's a chopper," yelled Harley above the unrelenting sound. Behind the white glare Cal could now see the outline of a black helicopter.

"Turn back!" a mechanical voice ordered. "You have entered a restricted area. Turn back!"

"Man, do it. Do it!" Cal said excitedly.

Harley obliged, sending the jeep around on the road in a cloud of dust. The helicopter buzzed their rear as if nudging them along.

"Man, he's still on our tail. Looks like something out of a sci-fi movie. Wait, there he goes. *Hasta la vista.*" Cal waved.

Harley drove back to where the road met the highway.

He stopped abruptly and took her in his arms. "There's something about this desert," he said.

"Maybe they're still watching," Cal reminded.

"Let 'em watch," Harley said. "Maybe they'll find out there's more to life than driving a big bad helicopter and scaring normal people to death."

"That man in the bar said you were an alien," Cal noted.

"C'mere," said Harley, "and I'll show you something out of this world."

24

"**EYE IN THE SKY**," Cal mumbled into the pillow, and punched it, shifting to get more comfortable. What morning light there was, coming through the bottom of the curtain, indicated that either it was very early or a storm was imminent.

Cal looked around and noted the bed's rumpled sheets and the fact that she was alone. Slowly the events of the night before came back to her.

"Harley? Harley?" she called out in a low voice made even deeper from sleep. There was no response save the sound of a faucet's steady drip. She got out of bed and went over to the bathroom's ancient sink and tried to shut it off but to no avail. She was in Harley's room back at the same motel she and Denny were staying at, not surprisingly since it was the only show in town.

She knew what she would see if she looked outside: the brown rental car, which they had picked up on their way back, and an empty parking slot where Harley's jeep had been. He was history. If it weren't for the empty condom packages, perhaps she could even think she had dreamed it all and he had been Harley, Desert Fantasy.

Wasn't this what she professed to want anyway? Wasn't this the scenario she asserted to find terribly erotic? Cal Brantley, Anyguy's woman—in control, sexually assertive, truly wanting only sex and viewing any emotional entanglement as encumbering.

Damn, that dripping water was annoying. Cal picked up her red dress and put it on, looking around for her panties. She had worn the dress with her hiking boots last night. Harley hadn't noticed or maybe it was that out here the combination was natural. Cal put on her socks and the boots, shot a look at herself in the pitted motel mirror, and peered both ways out of the window before opening the door. She had one hand on the doorknob before the thought buzzed at her again.

Eye in the sky.

There was a phone booth in the corner of the motel parking lot, she noted as she swung open the door.

"Is Mr. T. in?" Cal asked the receptionist back at the Reno casino. "This is Cal Brantley. Remember me? I was working on that accident involving the little boy."

"Cal, of course, I know who you are. Yes, Mr. T.'s in. I can connect you. Oh, by the way, you had a call this morning—"

"Is everything all right?" Cal said hastily; she was still not completely awake.

"I guess. He didn't leave a message. He said he worked with you. He had been told that you had checked out."

"Did he give you his name?" Cal asked.

"No. I told him you were out of town."

"Did you tell him where?"

"Well, yes, I did. But I told him you were expected back today. Was that all right? I mean—he said—"

"No, that's okay. It's okay, I'm sure." Cal was mystified. Orella knew she had stayed overnight in Rachel.

"Oh, one more thing, for what it's worth."

"Yes?"

"I noticed that the call came in on a house line. He was right here, in the casino, when he placed the call. I remember this because I probably would have been more cautious dispensing information if the call came in on an outside line. Well, I'll connect you to Mr. T. now."

There was a pause for a few moments, then the casino owner came on the line.

"Alex, it's Cal Brantley." Cal felt ridiculous standing out there in the red dress in the grungy phone booth in the run-down motel parking lot. At eight-thirty in the morning she felt as though she were going to a Halloween party on skid row.

"Cal, how is the investigation going?"

"Well, we're out here in Rachel and we interviewed that witness."

"What did he have to say?"

"I'm sorry, Alex, but I can't relay that to you. That information should come to you by way of the insurance adjuster."

"Right, you're right."

"I called because this idea came to me about the cameras in the casino. I realize they're focused on the tables. But I remembered the old system in the casinos was called 'eye in the sky' where casino security could look down over the entire scene. Are there any cameras that rove? Do you think any of them might have filmed the accident on the escalator?"

"No, I don't think so, Cal," he replied. Cal felt her hopes drop rapidly. "But let me think for a minute." There was a pause. Then Alex spoke again. "That aisle near the escalator leads directly to the cashier station. We always cover *that* area. Initially I had thought of the security cameras, but discounted the idea because I knew we didn't have one trained on the escalator. You're a genius, Cal!"

"How long do you save the tapes?"

"For up to a year. How will this help?"

"Well, it will memorialize the fact of the stroller being on the escalator. Also, I'm interested in seeing if anyone had that child by the hand."

"When are you arriving back in Reno?"

"We'll probably leave here in about an hour. I have to round Denny up for breakfast." *And I have to get out of this dress,* she thought.

"We'll have your rooms ready."

"Thank you, Alex."

"And perhaps dinner tonight, Cal?"

"We'll see how late we get in," said Cal.

Still no sign of Denny. The brown rental car was still where Cal had parked it last night. She wanted to shower before she faced her ever-vigilant partner this morning. She opened the door to her motel room.

Her bed was still made, clearly no one had slept in it. Cal looked around for her luggage; she was certain she had left it by the closet. Not there. She opened the closet door. Nothing. "What the—?" she said, holding her breath. The room was very small, and there was not a trace of her occupancy. She even checked her key number and then opened the door and made sure she was in the right room.

Denny's packed up the car already, she thought then. Well, he was just going to have to unpack it. She had to have a change of clothes before they hit the road. She had the case file in her black suitcase; she mentally made a checklist of what should have been in the room and what was missing. She always liked to pack herself, then she could make certain she had taken everything.

She went back outside. The door slammed; the wind was starting up again. High desert country was for the birds; and judging by the scarcity of even those, maybe it was fit only for the loners. And the aliens. How could you forget the aliens?

No one was in sight. Tumbleweed actually blew across the road the way it did in a low-budget spaghetti western.

"It's gettin-out-of-town time," Cal muttered. Then, without further hesitation she pounded on Denny's door. No answer. She peered in, trying to see if he was in there. There was a thin gap in the curtains. Cal closed one eye and peeped in. Now she was earning the stereotyped perception of her profession.

The bathroom door was ajar. No Denny in there, showering or otherwise. Most likely, thought Cal, he was at the breakfast place that they had discussed the day before. She turned to go, but then a nagging feeling made her take one more look.

She scrunched down and looked really hard inside the room. She couldn't see the head of the bed, but there, at the foot, was one of Denny's boots sticking out from the blanket. He *was* in there. Oversleeping, Cal thought crossly. At this rate they'd never get out of Dodge.

She began to pound on the door again. No response. Then she tried the doorknob. To her surprise, the door opened easily. It didn't lock automatically but had to be locked from the inside, when the occupant of the room was there. Denny didn't lock his door all night? What was with him?

"Denny, Denny," Cal called. He appeared to be completely under the covers, with only the one boot sticking out.

"Slept in his clothes," Cal muttered. "Maybe he's sick." She couldn't see his face, only the back of his head, blond hair looking neatly groomed even in sleep. "Damn helmet head," Cal said, wondering why she felt so nervous, so on edge.

She got up to the side of the bed.

"Denny," she called, much more loudly this time. He didn't stir. "Denny," she said, taking his shoulder gently and turning him a few inches.

Then, all her movements ceased. She stood as frozen in time as the ghastly tableau in the bed spread out before her.

Denny, the man who was armed with three guns. *

Denny, who noticed things like a fox.

Denny, the man who killed with his bare hands.

Someone had been there before Cal. In that godforsaken town that was a mere blip on the map, where only loners and nut cases and rattlesnakes were at home, where the wind blew you into the arms of strangers because the other alternative, being alone, became unbearable—someone had gotten to Denny.

Cal put a hand to her mouth, stifling the scream that wanted, ever so badly, to come out. Then she looked at her hand with undisguised horror.

She was smack in the middle of a crime scene. In this small, seedy room she could feel the loneliness now, full force. All that she had pushed away during the ride here, all that she had tried to ignore, to rise above, swooped at her. It brought its touch, its taste, its smell. Death was there, in that room, with her.

25

THE DAY WENT SWIFTLY downhill from there. If it were possible to go more downhill from finding your colleague murdered in his bed.

The Lincoln County deputy had set up a temporary command post in the Little A'Le'Inn. Cal's version of the last two days' events warranted an intensive debriefing, which, at this point in time, she was struggling to keep lucid, let alone succinct.

"Sure you don't want some coffee? Something to eat?" asked the deputy. Cal shook her head. The sight of Denny had been enough to rule out food in the immediate future.

"Now, Miss Brantley, let's go over this one more time."

"Officer Rutledge, sir, I'm afraid it will have to be the last that I can go over all this." Thoughts of Tony had been flashing in and out of her mind. Her head pounded. The urgency to locate him grew. Perhaps Denny's death was only a precursor of more to come. "I need to check out of the motel—"

"Let me remind you, Miss Brantley, that Denny Wickerstaff has checked out of that motel rather permanently. You are the last person to see him alive. No one else has any knowledge—"

"And I have no idea either who killed him!"

"We are taking this very, very seriously. Denny was one of ours, a fellow police officer, former-fellow officer—"

"I'm taking this very seriously too. I was the one who saw him—who discovered him—the body—"

"Exactly. Now tell us again about this Harley. No last name, you said?"

Cal felt like a total fool sitting there in that red dress and her hiking boots and not knowing Harley's last name. Maybe it wasn't even his first name. Yeah, come to think of it, he had been cool, real cool. And wait a minute—

"I just remembered something," Cal said suddenly.

The county cop sat up straighter. "Yes?"

"Harley said he was from L.A.," said Cal.

"And how does that help us?"

"Denny was from L.A." Cal didn't want to pin anything on Harley but she was trying to recall all that she could. "But Harley was with me all night," Cal insisted, trying to say something that would help him.

"You said you woke up and he was gone," reminded the deputy.

Cal picked at the hem on her dress.

"Someone really went at Wickerstaff with a vengeance," said Rutledge. "Sliced him with a maniacal intensity. Jealousy? Maybe. Robbery? Possibly. A crazy? We got some of those out here."

"That guy in the bar I told you about," said Cal, weakly agreeing.

"We've already picked him up. He's on his way in for questioning. Now, you say you were in town for a routine insurance investigation?"

"That's right. I'm due back in Reno tonight. They're expecting me."

"I'd be mighty careful traversing that desert country alone."

"The only alternative to that is staying," Cal said.

"But we got a killer on the prowl out there," said the cop, "and you should take precautions. That is, unless, you're not worried."

"Oh, I'm worried, I'm plenty worried."

"And your last interview last night was with—let me see if I've got this straight—a witch doctor?"

"No, that was a medicine woman."

"And she didn't have a name either." The cop made several scratching motions at his notepad. "Lots of people in this thing without names. Drunks, Harleys, witchy women."

"Surely you're familiar with Roy Comstock and his woman," Cal said. "I need to get going now," said Cal. "I want to make it to Reno before dark."

"Storm's comin' in too. They expected it to hit last night but it's comin' in. You got warm stuff other than that?" He motioned with a flip of his chin.

"You know, I almost forgot," said Cal. "I went to my room first. My luggage was gone. Why would they have taken that? I assumed Denny had gotten in there and put it into the car. Sometimes he's in a hurry . . . was in a hurry."

"It's hard, ain't it, thinkin' of the newly departed in the past tense? People have trouble with that, with their loved ones."

"Oh, I didn't love this guy, I only worked with him." Cal saw a trap now in every comment.

"I'll walk you to the car. See if Wickerstaff did pack it up. It might help us fix the time of death better."

Cal stood up like a jack-in-the-box. The officer was right at eye level with her and she was glad she wasn't wearing heels. He might want to lock her up if she were taller.

There was no one to see them stride down the three dusty streets to the motel parking lot. As they approached the brown rental, another white patrol car with a star on it and Lincoln County sheriff's insignia lurched to a halt beside them.

"This the man from the bar last night?" Deputy Rutledge asked.

Cal bent and looked inside the vehicle. The bum in the back seat regarded her back with dull eyes. In fact, they regarded each other with dull eyes. Cal turned away.

"Yes, that's him," she said simply. Rutledge nodded at the other deputy and the car sped off. Cal peered inside the brown rental. No luggage in the front or backseat.

"We both had car keys," Cal told Rutledge. "Let me just look in the trunk."

The trunk lid swung open. Empty.

"Looks like whoever killed your partner stole your luggage, miss."

"Great," said Cal. "And they've got all the work we did on that case. For what it's worth. Doesn't really matter, compared to the fact that Denny's dead."

"Well, what's this, what we got here?" exclaimed the officer, walking around to the front of the car and reaching under the windshield wiper. An object was stuck under the wiper and it appeared to be a washcloth, possibly from the motel. "Arghhh," he said suddenly, dropping it as if it were red hot.

"What the—?" Cal leaned forward to see what it was but he put up an arm to hold her back.

"Someone silenced your partner, miss. And then they had one final joke left to play. On you. Maybe they're waiting round to see your reaction. That's how some sickos are."

Cal looked around at the deserted street. Then she looked down at an object lying next to the washcloth in the dusty parking lot. Denny had had a vulgar and dirty mouth. But no more. Lying there, barely recognizable, was a human tongue.

26

THE SHERIFF'S DEPARTMENT HAD impounded her windshield wiper for further evidence testing and dusted the front of the rental car for prints. Then they had finally let her go. Back on the road, ghosts of memories rushed through her mind as the miles flew by.

She fed cassette tapes she had stashed in the glove compartment one by one into the player trying to keep her rage and fear at bay. The songs fed her recollections: Santana's "Singing Winds, Crying Beasts," making her recall the wind chimes at the medicine woman's house. George Michael's "Faith," reminding her of Harley's hands on her, that sly, laughing way he had of curling his lip when she'd speak her mind, tell her thoughts, scream out her pleasure. Madonna's "Sanctuary" and "Bedtime Story"—the aliens and their fondness for high desert country.

And she wasn't out of the woods yet.

The wind was really wailing now, she had to turn up the sound on the music. Blasting down the highway, dust and air and that white alkali powder rushing at her like a wind machine, a desert bobsled ride. She didn't look back.

Rutledge said the sheriff's office would notify Denny's next of kin. At some point, she'd have to call the office. Right now, she was drained and numb; it was going to take all her energy to get back to Reno. Carmen DeMille would be thrilled to learn that while the ongoing investigation was fairly successful, there had been a slight casualty. Her fair-haired boy. Someone hadn't taken to him. Who could it be? And if Cal had been in her own room, maybe they would have done more than just taking her luggage, like taking her life?

Or had Denny pissed off the great Comstock, the dabbling sorcerer/pseudowriter. Or his witchy woman? Was his murder tied in to the Violetta Fanny case or was it someone from his past? He had more than stepped on a few toes in his career at L.A.P.D. Hard to imagine they'd catch up to him in Rachel, Nevada, though.

Or Harley, going off like that, not a note. Not a word. The perfect fantasy lover—or demon?

Cal's mind spun with the different and terrifying possibilities.

A red light on the instrument panel suddenly went on. She was low on fuel. She had been in such a hurry to leave Rachel, she had forgotten to get gas. If Denny had been with her he would—if Denny . . .

She slowed down and fumbled at the map on the seat beside her. Hawthorne was the next town coming up; maybe she could make it.

Hawthorne. Red light. Red-light district.

Was Denny coming back from the dead in order to leave her a clue? About that, she had very mixed feelings.

Denny had hated the high desert country, Cal was thinking as she pulled into the gas station twenty miles later. She remembered how he had remarked he hadn't liked Highway 101 as they had headed out of the city. There hadn't been enough traffic for him. Well, the desert had been far worse for him. Torture, and more. Maybe he had known somehow—Cal wondered. He had been subdued that last day, not himself. Funny, she almost missed his biting sarcasm, his ribald anecdotes. His way of watching her every move. Had he really thought she was on drugs? And how much had he reported to the home office? She'd find out soon enough.

"Fillerup, miss?" asked the teenage boy coming around to the driver's window.

"What?" she asked with a start, unaware she had been just sitting there. She cautioned herself to be more on the alert about her surroundings.

"Fillerup?" he repeated, eyeing her red dress. She figured it wasn't the dress he coveted, unless the high desert did other things to men she couldn't imagine.

"You got that straight," she said, suddenly feeling she might burst into tears. She had heard that crying was therapeutic for grief, but not at a gas station.

The kid's cap threatened to blow off and he clapped a hand on it. "Wind's blowin' mighty strong," he commented, and then turned a vivid shade of red. "You'll be cold in that dress. I'll pump it for you," he said, and looked as if he were going to burn up with embarrassment. "No extra charge here for full serve." He gulped and then sputtered and coughed.

"Do you know how I get to Miss Kitty's Palomino Ranch?" asked Cal, not helping the situation any.

The whorehouse was circled by a chain-link fence as if it were an animal holding pen. It loomed out of the desert like a naughty mirage. Miss Kitty opened the door to the Palomino's front entrance as Cal stood there, her mind flipping around for a good pretext. She had to get inside the cathouse. All roads had led not to Rome but here.

Cal had told the Shoshone medicine woman she didn't have the questions. Now she had them; her mind fairly reeled with them.

Being a PI sometimes meant role-playing to get information. This was, unfortunately, one of those times.

Meanwhile the madam's eyes took the trip of her dusty outfit, from her hiking boots to the red dress, and up into Cal's eyes. Their gazes met, the madam's look was sultry and knowing, Cal's was defiant and strong. This was quite a stretch from the way Cal really felt now.

The madam's unspoken thoughts came hurtling at her with the once-over: *You're one of us,* it said, *no better, no worse. You're a member of the Losers' Club.* And Cal's mind screamed back: *You'll never get my mind or my body; I'll never sell out, either way.* Cal recalling reading something similar in detective fiction and now she was living it.

"What brings you to these parts, girl?" the madam actually drawled. Her outfit was vintage bordello, faintly reminiscent, Cal realized, of Carmen DeMille's office get-up. A large silver cross dangled between the madam's pushed-up breasts and instead of smacking of pious religion, it fairly reeked of sex and lust. Cal wondered how she had managed to pull that one off. A sign to the right of the door read Men Only.

"I hear tell you might have an opening for a new girl. Tuesday Hoele mentioned it to one of my friends. I've been trying to get off the street," said Cal. *I hear tell?*

"I can see that, hon, and none too soon, either. You look a bit the worse for wear," said the woman. "Tuesday ain't the best of references, but it'll do. All my girls call me Miss Kitty. You wouldn't look half bad cleaned up some." Her practiced eye roved over Cal. "How long you been a ho'?"

Two, three seconds, Cal thought. *Ho, ho, ho.*

"A year, maybe less."

"Hmmm," said Miss Kitty. "You got a habit?"

Sometimes I bite my nails. Cal was trying to keep it together, to strengthen her resolve. She thought then of Denny's tongue stuck under her car windshield wiper. Maybe that was too much resolution; she tried something else.

"Cat got yer tongue?" asked Miss Kitty, swinging the door open, wide open, to the Palomino Ranch.

Cal walked inside.

The girls were just sitting around and waiting. Cal, on the other hand, felt her mind and body moving at warp speed. *Time was running out,* she wanted to shout at them. They looked at her, eyes curious, nothing more. How did they see her—as competition? A possible friend? Or just one more working girl?

Cal nodded, strutting by them, slipping into her new role. Damn those hiking boots; how was she going to pull this off without some nice spike heels? *Pack the red dress,* she remembered Laurie saying as she pushed it into the suitcase. *Oh, Laurie, if you only knew how handy that dress would be.*

"Forms to fill out," said Miss Kitty, all business, showing Cal into a drab office. The entire place was rather disappointing in its decor. It looked as though they had either picked up the furnishings at a garage sale or they had been in business since the early fifties. Everything was Naughahyde, the walls wood paneling. Prostitution was legal in this area of Nevada and Miss Kitty had her business license framed on the wall along with several health notices and workers' comp information. Now here would be a great new client, thought Cal.

"Show you around after you get these completed," said the madam, appraising Cal with a connoisseur's eye. "You got yourself any other duds?" she asked diplomatically.

"My luggage was stolen," said Cal sadly.

"Hmmm," said Miss Kitty. "Well, I'm certain we can round you up some clothes. The other girls will have some stuff they can part with. We work as a team here, I won't allow it any other way. You get my drift?"

"I'm a team player, Miss Kitty," said Cal with a tiny leer.

"I don't believe I caught your name, girl." Miss Kitty

batted her eyes at Cal; she must have been quite a dish in her day.

"Cal," said Cal.

"Short for?"

"Cal . . . istoga."

"You can read and write, Calistoga?" Miss Kitty looked at her holding the pen but not filling out the form.

Cal laboriously wrote a big C on the space where it said name. "I've been to school, Miss Kitty. Never did quite get the hang of it, though. Sort of what led me to my current profession, I guess."

"Well, I'll let you fill out those forms and then I'll show you around." Miss Kitty wasn't going to sit there for the hour it took Cal to fill out the paperwork. She bustled out; as soon as the door closed behind her Cal jumped up and went to the file cabinet.

The file on Tuesday Hoele was not thick, mostly medical examinations and board of health certificates. Cal rifled through it, searching for the original employment application, like the one Miss Kitty had left for her to fill out.

Cal didn't know what she had expected to find, but she knew that if she saw it, maybe some of the pieces of the puzzle that made up the boy's death on the casino escalator would perhaps start to fit together. Why was Tuesday Hoele with him? Why were his fingers broken and never set? And why was his birth certificate a fake?

Here was something. Hoele gave a residential address in

Virginia City for a mailing address. Her permanent address was in Manila. Cal recalled the piece of property listed for Violetta Fanny in Virginia City. She couldn't remember the exact numbers, but the two street names were identical.

Cal nervously looked up once at the door as she began to thumb through the file cabinet again. She was in the *D*s. This was a long shot, but she wanted to be thorough. *That waitress at the casino who was murdered, Dawn, last name with a* D, Cal was thinking. *We need to see if there's a—*

Connection.

Cal pulled out a folder with Dawn Delaney written on it. Tuesday Hoele and the murdered woman had worked at the same place. Was Tuesday connected to her murder as well? And Denny. Cal shuddered.

Voices outside the door. Cal closed the file cabinet quickly. No one came into the office.

One more question, one more item to check out. And this was the difficult one. She looked in the three remaining file cabinets and then went over to the computer. She quickly switched it on and got into a folder marked Preferences. The little black book had gone the way of CD roms. There was Royce Comstock's name. Cal highlighted it.

The man was not only kinkier than she could ever have imagined, but Tuesday Hoele was one of his favorite girls. Cal thought back to when she had questioned him about knowing the Filipino woman standing in back of the boy on the escalator. An association Roy had denied.

They were all there that day in Reno: Violetta, Tuesday, Roy Comstock, and his medicine woman.

Cal clicked off the computer and walked back over to the file cabinet. Perhaps she had missed something. She re-opened the drawer and got out Tuesday Hoele's file.

"Who are you?" The sharp voice made Cal start and turn around. One of the girls from the front parlor stood at the office doorway. Cal didn't respond.

"Why you gettin' in those files for? You stealing? There ain't no drugs in there."

"I'm not looking for drugs." Cal found her voice.

"What's going on? Maybe I should get Miss Kitty." The girl was pretty but thin. Her long black hair was permed and the ringlets hung down nearly to her waist.

"I like your hair," said Cal.

"Well, thanks." She looked pleased at the compliment. "But I think you better come clean and tell me what's going on."

"Okay. I will tell you," said Cal. She stepped away from the cabinet. "I'm here looking for information."

"You're not here for a job?" The girl looked confused. "Miss Kitty said—"

"No. I only said that so I could get in here. Actually, I'm a private investigator. I almost never tell anyone that."

"A girl PI. Well! I thought only men did that kind of stuff." She looked at the filing cabinet and then back to Cal. "So, you on a case?"

"It's sort of confidential. You know? I'd like you not to tell anyone you saw me."

"Would that mean I was working on the case too?"

"We have people all the time help out, come forward,

give information. People who don't like to see bad things going on," said Cal.

"As long as Miss Kitty doesn't find out. I don't want to get fired."

"I just need some information," said Cal. "This woman, Tuesday Hoele, you know her?" Cal held up the file.

"She in some kind of trouble?"

"You two friends?" Cal asked cautiously, not wanting to make the situation worse.

"Her and me? No way. She's a skank, that one. I steered clear of her. She's gone, out of here now, and good riddance to bad rubbish. She came by yesterday to pick up her last check."

"Tell me about her," said Cal. "In thirty words or less," she added, eyeing the door.

"Aside from being a dirty bitch scum, I'd never turn my back on that one."

"That good," said Cal with a smile.

"That bad," said the girl. "She and another girl here got into a catfight over a customer. Miss Kitty was fit to be tied. I tell you, I never heard her get so pissed. That Tuesday ho', she sent the other girl to the hospital."

"Wow," said Cal, "what did she do to her?"

"Cut her, cut her real bad. That Tuesday Hoele, she loves to cut on people." Now it was the girl's turn to look toward the door apprehensively. "And there was something else—" the girl started to say, and stopped, clearly uncomfortable.

"Tell me," Cal urged. "This could save someone's life."

"Really? Whose life?"

"Hurry," urged Cal. "She's going to be back any second."

"There was a rumor going round, only a rumor. . . ." The girl hesitated.

"I'll take any kind of information, I'm not proud," Cal said.

"Tuesday was involved in some kind of a kiddie porn ring, out of the country somewhere—bad stuff, real bad—but . . . you're not going to go to the police, are you? I'll deny I said anything."

"No, I'll keep you totally out of this. Now—"

The door opened suddenly and Miss Kitty swept into the room. She walked over to where Cal's application was and looked down at it with dismay. "Well, Cal, you haven't gotten much filled out."

"Miss Kitty, I think I've changed my mind about working here," Cal said, making just the smallest movement toward the door.

"Oh, was it something Marta said?" The madam's cross bobbed angrily against her chest, again reminding Cal of her supervisor at Worldwide. The thought made her resolve stronger.

"Oh, no, Marta's been nothing but friendly. I just think you couldn't pay me enough to work here," said Cal. Now she was at the door, staring right into Miss Kitty's angry eyes, which looked really used up and old under all that black eye makeup. Then Cal was out in the hallway, heading toward the front door. Marta looked as if she were going to ask her if she could come with her. She looked back once. Miss Kitty had Marta by the shoulder.

"Everybody has their price, Cal," she said.

If she said anything more, Cal didn't hear. She was out of there.

27

SHEER NERVOUS ENERGY ENABLED Cal to complete
the drive back to Reno. The storm had subsided and when
she saw at last the city lights, they were clear and sparkling
like diamonds. It was late, but when she arrived at the casino
hotel's registration desk, she was expected. She had to tell
the clerk Denny wouldn't be using his room. Ever.

This time Alex had a suite ready for her. Two massive
bouquets awaited her arrival. A note from the casino owner
was on the desk along with a videocassette tape.

The immaculate upscale room contrasted sharply with the
way Cal looked and felt. If her outfit had looked outlandish
in Rachel and at Miss Kitty's, now it was downright bizarre.
She wanted to jump not only out of the clothes she wore
but out of her own skin.

In the marble bathroom was a luxurious velour robe. Cal
showered and wrapped it around her. Then she went to the
fully stocked bar and made herself a White Russian.

The video was the one showing the accident. It was the

third time she had watched the two-and-a-half-minute tape but she pressed rewind and hit the start button. She leaned forward in the cushiony sofa and raptly watched again.

What is wrong with this scene? she asked herself. *If I was a film director what would I do differently? My actors are too wooden,* she noted. *Emote, emote, show a little emotion. Especially you, there, big blond mom.*

What if that was my child? Cal asked herself.

If that was my little boy, I'd have him by the hand. Maybe little boys, they don't want to be held on to. But I'm the mother and what I say, goes. He's only four, after all. Okay, so the kid doesn't want anyone holding him, ever. And I know this going down the escalator. He makes such a scene usually I let him be. But then he's stuck, his jacket string is stuck. I see it. I get down on my knees and yell for help. I try and keep calm, for his sake, but I need help. I pull and pull and maybe with that superhuman strength I've heard sometimes mothers get in times of emergencies, I rip him loose. That's my kid there, my little boy.

Cal watched Violetta Fanny's face over and over.

She saw Tuesday Hoele coming down after them, holding that bag.

What an unlikely duo.

She watched Royce Comstock running toward the boy with his sharp hunting knife.

She saw Justin, the pit boss, at first unsuspecting, then as the full knowledge of what was happening hit him.

She watched it over and over again.

Tuesday Hoele coming down that escalator, the large birthmark on her face like a monstrous evil third eye.

She pressed rewind and watched it all again.

28

THE FIREBIRD TOOK THE turns heading up Highway 341, pine trees dotting orange hillsides, falling rock signs announcing life's precarious nature. Cal had turned in the brown rental car with its missing windshield wiper. Now, she read the road signs dutifully: Storey County Line and Geiger Summit elevation 6,789.

"Man, we are high, we are high," she said aloud. She felt alert and sharp after some sleep, breakfast, and a new pair of cheap jeans. "Lousetown Road," she read aloud, "wonder how they picked that name."

Virginia City sat up on a ridge surrounded by mountains. The highway let out right onto the main street imaginatively named C Street. She started to slow down when she saw she was within the city limits. Right after the Virginia City RV Park was a very small and oddly placed sign that Cal thought said Courthouse with an arrow to the left. She quickly turned left, wondering why the court was so close to an RV park. Two minutes later, another sign, which she was able to see more clearly, read instead Cemetery. She was lost.

The street dead-ended on a ridge that overlooked the town a short distance away. Handwritten lettering spray painted on a rock read Boot Hill. An official county placard read No Admittance after Dark.

Cal stopped her car to take a stretch and admire the magnificent vista. Not one for cemeteries and their quaint gravestones, she was drawn by the location's unusual ambience and, perhaps, her state of mind.

"Wouldn't catch me here after dark," she said to a man and woman who were heading for their car in the parking lot. The man had a camera around his neck. "Is this really Boot Hill?" she asked.

"These are the Silver Terrace Cemeteries," he responded.

"Is there a Boot Hill?" Cal wanted to know.

"Way I understand it, they told us in town, everybody's buried here. Miners, gamblers, gunmen, and just plain folks," said the man.

"And wanderin' around here after dark, you could meet up with a ghost," said the woman.

"Ghosts are good for business." The man gave a short laugh. "Tourism. Make a buck any which way they can."

"Maybe there's vandalism after dark," said Cal thoughtfully.

"And ghosts," said the woman. She was convinced.

The couple continued to their parked car, leaving Cal alone. She walked into the cemetery, looking out over the hills and the surroundings. The gravestones reminded her of Tony and his current situation; she hoped Orella had some further information and leads. Her mind spun with worry and concern. This graveyard was a warning of her failure to find him.

She began to feel more agitated, and walked around, glancing at the headstones. There was a miner killed as a result of a fire in the Gould and Curry Mine. A wife of the Storey County assessor killed in the rollover of a stagecoach. A spiritualist, who had "gone to join those who had gone before."

" 'Joining those who had gone before.' " Cal read it over again. Without looking around further, she hurried back to her car.

The statue of Justice over the main entrance to the Storey County Court House was without her usual blindfold. Cal looked up at the majestic masonry and felt inspired. Maybe it was time to take off her own set of personal blinders.

"Yes," said the clerk, "that file you ordered from storage is in. I thought Joe was going to pick it up."

"Well, he's working the case for me," Cal said. "But I'm in town so I thought I'd just stop by."

"Here it is," said the clerk, handing Cal an extremely thin folder.

"That's it?" said Cal, clearly disappointed.

The clerk nodded. "Just a small claims action. Another three months and that little guy would be purged. Better take what you can get."

"Isn't that the truth," Cal agreed.

"Copy machine in the corner, and no file materials should leave this room," the clerk said by rote.

Cal nodded and took the slim file over to a desk where she proceeded to look through it.

Violetta Fanny had been sued by a dental office for thirty-five dollars. Eventually the action was dismissed. Cal felt her hopes deflate, but she wrote down the name of the dentist anyway along with his phone number.

She made a quick drive-by of Fanny's Virginia City property. The house was on a small lot, down off the main street. There were no cars parked in the driveway or in the front. The blinds were drawn and on the second story, the curtains were in place. A wadded-up newspaper lay on the walkway to the front porch. The mailbox was situated at the curb but Cal didn't dare stop to check it. She cruised once to the end of the next block, made a U-turn, and at a normally slow speed, did one more look-see. Nothing in the backyard, not a plant or chair. No boats, no bicycles, no sign of life.

"I'm so sorry, but Dr. Davidson is out to lunch now," said the woman at the front desk, pushing the remains of her own nearly finished sandwich off to one side. "Is this a dental emergency?"

Cal inwardly winced. "Actually, perhaps you could help me," she smiled, although she felt like doing anything but. It looked like traveling to Virginia City would turn out to be nothing more than a wild-goose chase.

The lady smiled back, showing perfect teeth.

"I've been looking into an insurance matter," Cal said, and brought out the notes she had made regarding the small-claims court case. "Several years ago, your office sued a Miss Violetta Fanny. I found the case under public record. I know you probably don't remember, or perhaps you weren't working here then?"

"Actually, I do recall. Thirty-five dollars, wasn't it?"

Cal made no effort to hide her amazement. "You have an incredible memory," she said. "I'm Cal, by the way."

"I'm Alana Davidson. The doctor's wife. And actually my memory's not all that great. I just remember this because it was a mistake and so embarrassing."

"Could you tell me what happened?" Cal's curiosity was piqued; the woman seemed so uncomfortable.

"Well . . . you say you're looking into an insurance matter?"

Cal nodded.

"Mrs. Fanny, Violetta, did not show for an appointment. Automatically she was billed for the visit—that's our policy. She never paid. Then we had a temp for twelve weeks; I took off when I was giving birth to our second child. And the temp filed an action in small claims along with several others that we were trying to collect on at the time."

"Why do you say it was a mistake? Didn't she owe the money?" asked Cal.

"Well . . . I guess I can discuss this, it being public record and all. Actually, this shouldn't have been pursued, the amount being so small. And . . ." here the dentist's wife hesitated.

"And?" Cal prodded with a grin.

"You're not from around these parts," Mrs. Davidson said. "You see—you just don't mess with Violetta."

Cal said nothing this time, letting Mrs. Davidson go with her own flow.

"I don't really know her all that well. She graduated from school some ten years before me. But everyone knew—they said—that you didn't get in this woman's way."

"Are there any incidents that you might know of?" asked Cal.

Mrs. Davidson's eyes got round and worried looking as she listened to the question. "That was the house we, the neighborhood kids, avoided at Halloween," she said softly, looking downward.

"You were afraid," Cal prompted.

"She was the holiday spirit gone bad. She was the stuff of nightmares. The kids, the older kids, had told us she killed little children. That if you went into her house, you were never seen again."

"I think every neighborhood has their places and people to avoid," said Cal with compassion. "When I was growing up there was this one little old man—he screamed at us all year. At Halloween, no one would go to his house. We'd see his silhouette behind the curtains, waiting, with this bowl in his hands. The older kids told us the bowl was filled with worms."

"Maybe he was just lonely," said Mrs. Davidson.

"You know how kids are; no one would dare give him a chance," said Cal.

"Sometimes, I felt sorry for her, for Violetta. But then, other times, I just steered completely clear. Her parents were the original odd couple," Alana went on. "Very, very strict with her. And they looked like the couple in that painting, 'American Gothic.' "

"Did Violetta have any children?" Cal asked.

"One, I think," said the dentist's wife, casting an eye at the office clock. "Well, anything else . . ."

"I thank you for your time. You've been very helpful."

"I hope it helps your insurance matter. Oh," she added as Cal turned to go, "there's someone who might be able to give you a bit more information. Mrs. Olsen, the former principal at Virginia City Middle School. She's getting on in years, but she's sharp as a tack. Here's her address." Mrs. Davidson copied it from her Rolodex. "She lives right on D Street across from the school grounds."

The weather had started to turn brisk and the children playing out in the schoolyard were wearing jackets. Their laughter and excited voices carried across the street as Cal found the house matching the number she had been given.

"Mrs. Olsen?" she asked the elderly woman sitting in a rocker on the porch.

"Heard you comin', don't have to shout at me," said the lady sternly. She turned her face toward Cal. Her eyes were filmy with cataracts.

"Sorry, I thought maybe I had to be louder than the noise the kids are making," Cal said.

"That's not noise. You think that's noise you don't know the meaning. That's music. I know you?"

"No, I'm not a former student, Mrs. Olsen. One of the townspeople sent me over to see you; she said you were a town historian."

"Get old, you become a historian. You have a name?"

"I'm Cal, Cal Brantley. Pleased to meet you," Cal shook the woman's wrinkled hand. Her grip was surprisingly strong.

"Good manners. Someone did a good job of raising you."

"My mom was a hippie. She practically lived in Golden Gate Park," Cal remarked.

"Always be proud of your roots. She was what she was, who she had to be, just like you are."

Cal thought about this for a minute, then decided to accept it as wisdom. "Funny, I never quite thought of it that way," she admitted.

"Wait till you have children. I never had any, but these"—she motioned with her hand—"are the kids of my kids."

"Mrs. Olsen, I'm looking into a matter concerning insurance and I wanted to ask you about a Violetta Fanny."

"Hmph." The old woman shook her head. "Always wondered when someone would be around to ask me about that one. Insurance, you say?"

"Yes," replied Cal.

"I'll take you at your word, young lady. You have a good,

strong, honest voice. I could always tell the liars. I was good at that."

"I bet you were."

"Oh, I was. No one got away with anything. Yes, and that incident, that bad time, years ago, with Violetta. No one got away with what happened—what they did. Not that it helped her any. Ruined her."

"Would you tell me what happened, Mrs. Olsen?"

"Sit yourself down, I'm too old to yell upwards. I keep yellin' thataways, God'll be thinkin' I'm callin' to Him."

Cal sat down.

"Well, it was many years ago, thirty-five or so, I'd reckon. Yep, seems that would be about right. That Violetta Fanny, she was an unhappy girl, even before the trouble. Parents ruled her with an iron hand. Too hard on her. Remember, Cal, be firm with your children and consistent. But don't forget to show affection. That's an important part of love."

"I'll remember, Mrs. Olsen."

"Good girl. Well, Violetta was an ugly girl. Tall, too tall for a woman, feet like beaver traps. Rigid, unfriendly set to her mouth. I see that face like it was yesterday. Not a bad student, parents wouldn't let her be. But unhappy. So unpopular. You've got to have balance in your life. Remember that, Cal."

"I will, Mrs. Olsen. I try."

"You young people. You all work too much. That's not good, Cal."

"Yes, Mrs. Olsen."

"Well, one day this group of boys was ribbin' Violetta.

And she suddenly ups and smacks one. Knocked out his front teeth. They had been ribbin' her for some time, you see. Then, him and his friends, they waited up for her after school."

The woman paused.

"What happened, Mrs. Olsen?" Cal found she was holding her breath.

"Violetta always walked home with the shortcut. Near the edge of the blackberry tangle. Well, this time the boys they lit out after her, surrounded her. Way she told it, they attacked her. Her face got cut up, something awful."

Cal thought then of the big blond's scarred face, the cuts that crisscrossed her skin.

"That's not all," Mrs. Olsen said, although she looked as though she didn't relish continuing. Cal waited and didn't say a word.

"They raped her," Mrs. Olsen said all at once. The children's yells from the schoolyard came from the distance but neither Cal nor Mrs. Olsen spoke for a few minutes.

"The boys said they didn't rape her. That she had been takin' them back there, near the tangle, for some time. Lettin' them have their way with her. They admitted they had chased her that afternoon and she had fallen into the tangle.

"I had no choice at the school. They were expelled. The three of them."

"You believed her, then?" asked Cal.

"I didn't have a choice. The boys were convicted in a court of law and sent to reform school."

"Convicted," repeated Cal.

"Violetta was pregnant. She had the baby."

"Is that her only child?" said Cal.

"Far as I know. After she gave birth, her parents said that the doctors told them Violetta could never have children again. Or maybe they had her—fixed." Mrs. Olsen spoke the terrible words as if they made her physically sick. She passed a hand over her eyes and shook her head. "Baby died that next year. Pneumonia," said Mrs. Olsen gravely. "They chased her, she said. She got that face all scarred up. Ugly on the outside. But Cal, you mark my words. That Violetta, she was messed up way worse before that happened, on the inside. Know what I mean?"

"I think I do, Mrs. Olsen. I think I do."

They sat for a few minutes without speaking again, the old principal and the young investigator, each lost in her own thoughts.

"You come and see me again, Cal. All my children do," said the old woman.

"I will," promised Cal, "whenever I'm in town."

"Where you from, Cal?"

"San Francisco."

"You're a far ways from home."

"Not so far. I'll come and visit."

Mrs. Olsen was silent then, she didn't speak again, but instead turned her head toward the schoolyard. Recess was over and the children had filed into the classrooms. A teacher had walked to the fence and was picking up two jackets that had been left on the ground. Cal watched as he looked inside the collars.

Name tags, Cal realized. *He was checking for name tags.*

<u>29</u>

"WE'VE GOT SPIRITS, DEAD spots, apparitions, and strange energies, but no phone. Sorry," said the man at the Hill House Bed and Breakfast.

"Make sure I get a room without spirits," Cal said earnestly. "I've had contact with the recently departed."

"It can be hair-raising," agreed the man.

"Well, he was still alive," said Cal, "but now I don't want to take any chances."

"We've got all the ghosts we can handle right now," the man said honestly. "Here's the key for number four. And I think you'll find a pay phone right next to the Bucket of Blood Dead Wagon. Can't miss it."

"I just love this town," said Cal.

"I just want you out of there," said Orella.

"You're not my supervisor," Cal argued.

"They got to him, an armed ex-cop. What do you think they'll do to you?"

"I think they got what they wanted. The case notes," said Cal, munching on some popcorn.

"Where are you now?"

"I'm right outside the Bucket of Blood saloon."

"This is—this is insane, Cal. What can you hope to prove? That casino owner doesn't care. Maybe his premium will go up next year. He'll write it off."

"Orella, you're so pragmatic. I need to finish what I started. I can't leave it with loose ends."

"The only thing loose is you—you're a loose cannon."

"Compliments will get you everywhere."

"Promises, promises."

There was a brief silence.

"I got into the system one more time. For you," said Orella a bit more resentfully.

"You don't want to help save a human life?" asked Cal.

"Not this one," said Orella.

"Let me tell you," offered Cal. "There was a credit card charge in Virginia City. Today."

"Are you psychic?"

"No."

"How did you do that? What a parlor trick! Or only coincidence?"

"Long car trips. And there are no coincidences. Know it."

"You're good."

"Believe it," said Cal, "and don't worry so much."

"But you got to know when to fold," warned Steve.

"I'll walk away when it's time," promised Cal.

• • •

Cal felt hungry and filled with nervous energy. She started to walk but the plank sidewalks on the main street seemed to trip her up. She went back to the car and started to drive. She didn't see any likely looking place to get a meal as she went from one end of the town to the other. Then she spotted a restaurant called the Wagon Wheel and thought maybe that would be okay. She had missed the entrance to the small parking lot and had to circle round the block. She made the turns and was heading back when she saw she was only one block from Violetta Fanny's house. Curiosity forced her to cruise by. No cars. No lights. But then she noticed that the newspaper was gone from the front walkway.

30

NIGHT HAD FALLEN, SUMMONING a western sky studded with rhinestone stars. The days were growing shorter, Cal thought as she looked upward.

She had been cocky and daring on the phone with Orella, but that had all been a put-on, a false bravado. It was cold and dark as she passed under the Silver Terrace Cemetery archway and she actually longed for a companion. This was a bad place to be alone as the moon drifted over the tombstones and their occupants gave silent promise to give up their mysteries.

Cal walked deeper into the cemetery.

The day-trippers had left the tourist haunts and the town lights were blinking out faster than a spinster's bedside lamp. Cal drifted around the pathways, once in a while taking out her penlight to read an inscription. There wasn't much else to do while she waited.

The moon came out, a ghost of its former self a few nights ago, and rose hesitantly in the sky. Light mist began to roll in from the lower valley floor and swirled around the cemetery plots.

Time went by very slowly; it could do as it willed up here, seemingly capricious in duration. Good times flew by, bad times lasted endlessly. This was one of those endless times. Fate was such a gagster.

Cal heard the crunch of gravel nearby. She stopped all her movement and listened closely. There it was again. Slipping and sliding it drew closer. Mice? Rats? Unsleeping dead?

She drew a big breath, and then clearly said, "Tony? You can come out now."

There was no response. It grew very still again, real still, and Cal could feel the skin crawl on her arms. Maybe this had not been such a cool idea. She began to walk back to the car. What was that? It sounded like a cough. Did ghosts cough? Wasn't death a cure for the common cold?

She almost called out Denny's name but stopped herself. That would have been totally geeky. *Keep it together Cal*, she warned herself, *you're coming undone.* "You're good," Orella had told her. *I'm good,* she told herself now. It was an excellent time for an old-fashioned pep talk.

She kept walking toward where she thought the parking lot was situated, but the mist had quickly turned into fog and whatever town lights there had been had disappeared. She lost her bearings. She recalled Harley had had a compass on his dashboard. Harley. She should totally forget about him. How cool he had been, just up and leaving her that morning. Mr. L.A. She was miffed because she was supposed to be the one who did the leaving. Miffed, no, that didn't cut it, stunned maybe. Humiliated, perhaps.

Face it Cal, your love life is an utter and complete fiasco.

What a great place for self-reckoning. Cal made a mental note to recommend it to everyone.

Gravel sounds again. A rock being kicked. That was it.

"That's it!" she called out loudly. "Get out in the open, Tony. Get the hell out or I swear I will never forgive you!"

And a minute later he actually did.

He looked pale and disheveled as though he had been ridden hard. A lock of black hair dangled down on his forehead and he reminded Cal of the unrepentant teenagers in the musical *Grease*.

"Have I ever told you that on some days you look like John Travolta?" she said.

His face brightened and with a pudgy hand he swiped at some beads of sweat that had formed on his forehead and threatened to trickle down his face.

"Then or now?" he said.

They were actually standing there, in that graveyard, and teasing each other. Just like old times. Well, not quite. They had eschewed graveyards as one of their teenage haunts, favoring parks instead.

"How did you figure it out?" he asked, stepping one step closer to her.

She stepped backward one step. "You knew I'd come after you," she replied simply. She stared at him unblinkingly.

"I want you, Cal," he said.

"It's over, Tony. It's been over."

"Give me a second chance."

"I need to know the truth, Tony. Tell me how far you were going to go on this?"

"You mean the suicide thing? Yeah, I could do it. I wanted to do it."

"You don't have to convince me, Tony. What I want you to get is help. You need professional help."

"Cal, please. Let me hold you. Let me touch you," his face was a mask of yearning.

"We need to talk," Cal said.

"We're talking now, aren't we?" He took another step forward.

"I'm working a case now, Tony. This cat-and-mouse game you've been playing—did you ever stop and think about the possible consequences?"

"I—I—"

Cal tried to go easy on him; she saw he was low, very low even for him. "The things I did to look for you, Tony—do you realize I put my career on the line?"

"What—you did?" He looked as if he were going to be sick.

"I want to help you, Tony. I never . . . never want anything to happen to you. You must know this and carry this knowledge with you. Forever."

"Forever." The word seemed to give him hope.

"But you must never play games with me again."

He swung his head back and forth like a moose. He gave her a sickly smile.

"This case I'm working on now here in Nevada—it's bad Tony, real bad."

"That's just it, Cal. You're doing things with your life. Meaningful things. And you're good at it. In fact, you're great. You are great. I want to be with you, Cal. Can you blame me?" He took several steps forward.

"Stop, Tony! We're talking now. Right?"

"We're talking." He looked totally disappointed. "It was the Old Players Club, wasn't it? That's when you first caught on?"

"You're not great at hiding in corners, Tony. That was you when those two jumped me in the ladies' room. Right?"

"I couldn't believe those lowlifes. Yeah, I took that guy out."

"And that wild-goose chase to the NAA meeting."

"I'm sorry, Cal."

"You called the casino office when you tried to see if I was in my room, but they told you I had checked out."

"Guilty."

"It all started at the anniversary party when you overheard me talking about my new case in Reno. You didn't figure on another investigator working on the case with me."

"Man, that dude!" Tony raised his voice a notch. "He ruined my plan, he—"

"Now we're in a jam, Tony," Cal said sharply, cutting him off.

"The case you're working on?"

"Yeah," said Cal.

"Let me help. You know I've helped in the past."

"Oh, Tony . . ." Cal paused and looked at a nearby grave. He started to walk toward her again. "Stop, Tony," she said sharply. "My God, look at this." She pointed at the tombstone and clicked on her penlight. Aloud she read: "Yes, she is gone and/we are going all/like flowers we wither/and like leaves we fall.

"Moira Fanny. Died age thirteen months." Cal passed a hand over her eyes.

"Do you know who she is?" Tony asked. Cal didn't answer, unable to speak for a minute. "Cal, I need to know—why here? Since you know I was following you and not the other way around, why did you come here?"

Cal looked at him, tears starting in her eyes. "Look around, Tony. This is a graveyard. Is this what you want for yourself? Surely there can be another answer for you. This is so final."

"I think I see."

"Do you? It could be a start."

"I want to start over Cal, with you. There's nobody else I want. That's part of it. I want you. I've never met another woman who is so comfortable with being herself. You let your bra straps show."

Cal smiled at that. "Well, they're not showing now. I'll help you, Tony. But you must never pull a stunt like this again."

"Tell me about this case, Cal. Let me help."

"Man! I can't see what I ever saw in you. Were you this much of a brute as a teenager?"

"Worse." Tony was smiling now.

"You just wear away at a person."

"Let me be around you, Cal. I feel much better when I'm around you."

"We're going to get you help, Tony. You hang in there."

"This person"—he motioned toward the grave—"you know who she is, don't you?"

"I'm not certain of all the angles, Tony. Nothing I can prove yet either. But I'm pretty sure that they've got planes coming in, probably bringing dope and landing on the dry lake beds down near Rachel. Then they're flying out kidnapped kids."

"Cal, Cal." He was suddenly right next to her. His arms went tightly around her; she was squashed in his embrace.

"No way! Don't!" She tried to get her mouth out from under his. She struggled fiercely in his grasp. His kiss was hot and long. She screamed but there was no one to hear but him. They kept struggling. Then she kicked him. Hard.

He went sprawling.

"Dust to dust," he moaned, holding his leg.

"Dirt to dirt," she responded. "I warned you. You never listen."

"I think I'm going to need knee surgery."

"Serve you right."

"Help me get up."

"No way, you're not on your best behavior."

"I promise."

"Damn you," said Cal, and gave him a hand. Then they both heard it. Over the sound of the wind's moans came the crunch of gravel. Cal and Tony looked at each other with surprise and fear.

A huge shadow loomed over the nearby grave.

Cal looked up, right into the face of Violetta Fanny.

"A monster," whispered Tony.

31

No Coincidences.

Cal smelled the dirt and felt the wind and heard it rush on its way to another destination. Would these be the last things her senses felt? Dying in a cemetery. How convenient.

She thought in a rush about the woman who had died in the stagecoach rollover. How death comes for you and sometimes you didn't know it was going to be your time. But the reaper picks his own hour.

"Violetta," said Cal, trying to keep her teeth from chattering.

"You know this—this—" said Tony, his voice quavering.

"The woman in the case," said Cal.

Tony got to his feet and rushed at Violetta Fanny. "Kidnapper!" he yelled like a warrior. Then he clutched at his knee and staggered. Violetta stepped forward and took a backhanded swipe at him. Tony went down like a fly, hitting his head on the corner of a tombstone. Cal rushed over to him, ignoring Violetta. She made sure Tony was still breathing.

Cal stood up. The woman was massive, and somehow, out here in the open, in the dark with the fog and the wind, she seemed even bigger. Smash and break; Cal vainly tried to recall the martial arts video. But this was like David and Goliath. What could she use? She needed something more.

"He hurt you," said Violetta almost apologetically, "so I hurt him."

"No, he wasn't hurting me," said Cal. The woman wanted conversation before she killed her.

"I saw—I watched. It was like them—the boys. What they did to me."

"That was many years ago, Violetta," Cal said in an even tone. She had her car keys out from her bag. She could use those. How to get to the giant's eyes though? Stepladder?

"Each night I come here to say good night to this baby," said Violetta. "I have a new baby now."

Cal stared at her in wonder. Was the woman putting her on? Toying with her? Tony moaned. That was good.

"Violetta. That is not your baby. That is someone else's child. Here is your baby." Cal motioned to the tombstone. "Violetta, I cannot even begin to imagine how bad that must have been for you." So bad she must have snapped.

"The baby is in my room," said the big blond, her eyes blank like a doll's.

"Then the babies leave, right, Violetta? Where do they go?" said Cal to keep her talking.

"They go on trips."

"They're stealing these babies, Violetta. Can't you understand? They're taking these babies away from their real mothers. Just think how you would feel?"

"Other mothers?" The woman looked confused.

"They're using you. Can't you see? They're using you and your house. As a cover."

"Tuesday is a bad woman?"

"You're not in on it!" Cal exclaimed. She looked at Tony, who had passed out again.

"Men are bad," said Violetta simply.

"Not all men," said Cal. "But your friend Royce Comstock, he's not so good. Along with his little witch. He's a bad man. All that writer garbage."

"Royce is a bad man?" The big blond shook her head.

"Who killed my partner? The man I came to your house with?"

"Royce said he and Tuesday sent him to heaven. He asked too many questions."

"Violetta, we've got to go to your house," Cal said urgently.

The big blond bent and picked up Tony as if he were a toy and slung him over her shoulder effortlessly. "I'll show you my room," she said.

32

VIOLETTA DIDN'T PARK IN the front of the house but instead pulled around the back onto a small dirt path. No neighbors' windows had vantage points to see behind the house and only a row of large mature trees stood witness. Violetta got out a ring of keys and unlocked the cellar door. Then she and Cal went inside; they left Tony, who was starting to come around, in the backseat of the car.

The house was pitch-black but Violetta made no movement to put on a light. Cal stood still for a minute or two while her eyes adjusted. Violetta held a finger to her lips and made a shushing motion. "Trick or treat," Cal muttered.

Cal trained her penlight on the steps as they went to the second floor. They passed by a room with a urine-soaked mattress on the floor. Cal had visions then of Violetta's childhood. She tapped the large woman on the shoulder. "Your room?" she asked. The odor made her gag.

Violetta shook her head. "My room," she said in a low voice and pointed toward a set of attic stairs. Cal had uneasy misgivings about being in the house alone with this woman, but then again, what choice did she have but to go along? No, Violetta didn't act as though she were putting her on.

But still Cal hesitated about going up those last set of stairs. She shivered at the thought of what could be up there.

"Violetta, how long did you have these babies with you?" Cal asked.

"For a while. 'Until people forget,' Roy said."

Cal thought of the too-small jacket.

"Why were you in the casino that day?"

"Roy came to take the boy for a ride. He said it wasn't good for him to come to the house."

Cal thought it out. They were in the casino to make the switch. The children were warehoused for months until some of the furor over their kidnapping had died down.

I go to Reno for supplies, Cal recalled him saying. *And diversion.*

"So he meets you in a crowded public place," Cal mused aloud.

"Too crowded," said Violetta. "The terrible accident." She shook her massive head. "My room," she said again, and nudged Cal with her elbow.

"Violetta." Cal was whispering though she didn't know why. "When this is over, you need to get some help."

"You help," said the large blond.

"I'd like to help you, but I mean—"

Suddenly there was movement in the dark behind them. Both Cal and Violetta turned. The Filipino prostitute stood there, a knife in her hand.

"Bad woman!" cried Violetta as Tuesday Hoele rushed at them. Violetta grabbed her hand as Tuesday drew it back to stab at Cal. *She likes to cut people.*

Tuesday and Violetta struggled as Cal looked around for something to smash over the woman's head. She didn't see anything. The knife thudded into the woodwork in back of her. Violetta grabbed for it, but the cheap handle broke off, leaving jagged naked steel.

Tuesday brushed her hair from her eyes and in the faint light that came through the second floor window from a nearby streetlamp, Cal could see the large ugly birthmark on the woman's face, staring at her like a third eye. Tuesday pulled out a straight razor and when the big blond rushed her again, she thrust her cutting hand upward and slit the blond's throat. Violetta's eyes closed; one brown, one blue.

"Now you," growled Tuesday, turning to Cal. The blade of the razor was dark with blood. She came at Cal without hesitation. Cal quickly unclasped Tony's heavy steel ID bracelet and with a powerful movement swung it across her attacker's eyes. The woman dropped the razor and held her hand to her face, covering her eyes. Then she stumbled hard backward against the wall, impaling herself on the broken weapon.

Cal ran up the attic steps and put her ear to the locked door, hearing for the first time a child's weak cry. Then she rushed back down the stairs, remembering Violetta's key ring. As she unlocked the door, she thought: *This was your room, Vi-*

oletta. What else did they do to you? The girl was lying on a small cot and she looked at Cal hopefully.

"You're somebody else's baby," Cal said softly, and reached forward to pick her up and comfort her.

I've had enough of danger
And people on the streets
I'm looking out for angels
Just trying to find some peace

—GEORGE MICHAEL

EPILOGUE

IT WAS OVER, ALL of it.

Cal was heading back down the hill toward the highway when she saw the strange animal by the side of the road. She could have sworn it was a large rabbit with horns like an antelope.

Instead of running across in front of her, it paused and stared back at her with large gray eyes. Their gazes locked and then it turned and ran back into the brush.

Cal was thankful that she hadn't hit it, and then questioned herself if she had even seen it correctly. Those horns! Those eyes! She didn't think an animal like that existed.

She looked heavenward and silently sent a thought: *Denny Wickerstaff—you're no angel!*